Some Things about Flying

that are
too _weird_.

Joanne + Dave

Some Things about Flying

JOAN BARFOOT

KEY PORTER BOOKS

Canadian Cataloguing in Publication Data

Barfoot, Joan, 1946–
      Some things about flying

ISBN 1-55013-908-8

I. Title.

| PS8553.A7624S65 | 1997 | C813'.54 | C97-931149-7 |
| PR9199.3.B371S65 | 1997 | | |

The publisher gratefully acknowledges the support of the Canada Council for the Arts and the Ontario Arts Council for its publishing program.

This novel is entirely a work of fiction. Any resemblance to persons living or dead is purely coincidental.

Key Porter Books Limited
70 The Esplanade
Toronto, Ontario
Canada M5E 1R2

Printed and bound in Canada

97 98 99 00 6 5 4 3 2 1

GRACELESS AND FLAILING, Lila hurtles through a long darkness deep and rhythmic as heart-beats.

She lands, hard and suddenly, in high shocking light so brilliant she briefly closes her eyes.

Inside her head, tiny jigsaw puzzle bits flung upwards, thrown sideways, fall disordered here and there.

She could lick black water from puddles, sweat from skin, ice from wings, blood from a stone.

She can't seem to hear, but her body vibrates to a kind of rumbling, and to a higher-pitched hum. Mouths close and open in faces with moisture rising off them like hope, forming a mist of desire. In this strange steaminess, she has trouble catching her breath.

Her heart hurts most, then her head.

But how swiftly she begins to quantify injury. What a foolish brain, that sets out so quickly to sort, analyse, file, put in place—she does have to laugh at herself. Although it's also familiar, a comfort, that as a companion, irony, at least, remains dependable.

. . . .

one

HERE ARE LILA AND TOM, going off on their holiday together at last. Since they are headed for something, a shared venture, an adventure, Lila observes the details of their progress with keen and superstitious, if also quite practical, interest, and imagines Tom does too.

They're both experienced travellers in their different ways and fields, and have packed with care. Also they have discussed what they may need, and what may be safely left behind, for two weeks in another country. "We don't want to be weighed down too much," Tom said, and Lila couldn't agree more. After waiting so long, and in her view so patiently, she has been looking forward to the weightlessness of freedom, anonymity, a refreshing carelessness, and doesn't care to lug along great piles of baggage.

In the end they each have a small carry-on bag and a large case, with a bare-bones range of clothes from hearty to festive. "Because we can always do laundry or drop stuff at a dry cleaner's," Tom said. Even sitting with Tom in a laundromat sounds fine to Lila. Even dropping off shirts and blouses mixed up together, on the same bill, feels luxurious.

For the journey itself, Lila has chosen sturdy beige shoes, light blue uncreasable pants and a beige sweater, a loose open weave that will let her skin breathe but keep her comfortable, too, if the plane's cabin is cool, as cabins sometimes are.

Tom turns up at her door flushed and nervous. He too has chosen a beige theme, although in slightly different format: beige cotton pants, darker beige cotton shirt, light brown shoes. Lila wonders if, despite everything, they may not be, in truth, a beige pair of people. That would be an awful disappointment.

"Ready?" he asks. "You look great."

She ought to; she actually spent last evening dyeing her hair back to what once was its natural light brown, covering creeping grey. An embarrassingly transparent thing to do, really. Struggling with the plastic gloves, mixing the ferocious, unfamiliar chemicals and colours, she considered whether this could be a step over some pathetic line: both revealing too much hope, and admitting to a soft and petty kind of discontent.

Still, it seemed a kind of good-luck thumbs-up for the trip, and somewhat transforming.

There was nothing last minute to be done about her pouchy warm belly, but then Tom has one of those, too, only his rides higher. They may no longer have perfect taut bodies, if either of them ever did, which she for one did not, but they do have matching ones. His bulges fit her nooks nicely, and vice versa.

Here are Lila and Tom, optimistic, middle-aged, pouchy lovers, going off on their holiday together at last. Definitely old enough not to imagine details and signs count for much. Nevertheless, everything from the moment he rings her doorbell is part of the journey, and has its significance.

Is it hard to find parking, and is there then a long wait for the airport shuttle that takes them to the terminal? No, these matters tick along efficiently. Are the lines in the terminal long? Not really; at least they're not the worst either has encountered on previous, separate journeys. Does the counter agent treat their luggage with less-than-complete abandon? Yes, and this also seems good, although as far as she knows neither is travelling with anything breakable, except their own crystal selves.

Lila, who is a professor of English, and who, more to the point and unlike some of her colleagues, does actually take pleasure in words, is slightly ashamed of that image: too obvious, and absurdly melodramatic. Still, while it's one thing to love words, she understands it's quite another matter for words to love back. An unrequited romance, it often enough has turned out to be. Or an unbalanced one.

When she and Tom reach the head of the departure line, is either of them carrying some inadvertent, mysterious metal that would send them back and forth through the detectors? Only Lila, and only once, because leaving home she stuck the ring with her house and car keys in the pocket of her slacks, without thinking. Tom waits patiently, kindly, a good sign.

They keep touching each other, reaching out to fingers, shoulders, the smalls of backs.

Even the flight is sharply punctual, a rare treat. And does the flight attendant smile? Oh yes, especially at Tom, but perhaps she recognizes him from days when he was better known. And the aisles and seats are clean, although they're certainly neither wide nor luxurious, not like business class, which Lila prefers for long journeys. "I can't afford to go business," Tom told her, although naturally he could. What he couldn't do is justify the expense to anyone else.

But economy is comfortable enough, and it's only, with luck and a tail wind, for seven hours or so. Lila and Tom are both accustomed to spending long periods sitting, and this is hardly gruelling, only cramped.

Neither of them has seen the in-flight movie, a nouveau Western they once mentioned renting. They may or may not watch it now, but it's another small, good sign.

Lila sighs happily and grips the armrests. She is tense at takeoffs, Tom on landings, so his armrest-gripping is hours in the future. She holds tight even knowing that if the takeoff were unsuccessful, which this one naturally is not, her rigidity, the way she has clamped her feet hard against the floor and pressed her back into the seat, would result in far more damage than if she were loose and relaxed. The way drunks often escape barely injured from quite serious accidents, too pie-eyed to react to fear.

Still, whatever her mind knows, her body goes its own disobedient way, as it tends to do in various matters.

Now they're up, now they're levelling off. They're away!

This is a moment which has been much imagined. Lila is slightly amazed that, as a moment, it is just as she imagined. They've been anticipating this journey for months, plotting and planning, talking and dreaming. Once, they rented *The Great Escape* for the title alone.

Tom's head falls happily against the back of his seat. "Goddamn, Lila, we did it. We're here."

It seems to her their desires fit as snugly as their nooks and bulges.

They plan to go first to a little London hotel Tom picked, near theatres and Covent Garden. "It's not luxurious by a long stretch," he told her, "but it's comfortable, and odd enough to be entertaining."

He will drop in briefly at a conference of Commonwealth historians, his excuse, reason, justification, whatever, for the trip. For the day or so he's there, Lila will sit in cafés drinking wine, walk across ancient bridges, rest on benches with her lunch, no doubt fending off pigeons. Then, once Tom has freed himself, they'll amble together through a great gallery or two, indulge in an extravagant dinner, before heading, fairly aimlessly, into the countryside.

"We could pretend we're an obscure branch of royalty," Lila suggested, "and be ridiculously pampered."

"I guess that rules out the plaid Bermuda shorts. And the Hawaiian shirt with the palm trees, and the camera on a strap around my neck."

"And the white belt, don't forget. I always think it's the accessories that make or break an outfit."

They've had such fun planning this. Their hopes, she feels, are huge.

There is, of course, the conference, a blip in the vision. "There're a few people I'd like to catch up with," Tom said, "and at least I have to make an appearance, but I'll get away the first moment I can." Certainly Lila understands there are prices to pay for such luxuries as time, and at least this sounds like a relatively minor cost.

She also understands that ordinarily, on his own, Tom would enjoy the conference, which is right up his alley and would give him a chance to meet, or re-meet, colleagues from all over the world; to discuss new economies, emerging movements, some contexts for disasters he only sees, these days, on television. The best part of such an occasion, and she knows this herself, is when delegates hang around hotel rooms and bars, exchanging stories and questions, hearing tales and ambitions that give genuine glimpses.

He still misses being so close to actual event that sometimes, he has told her, "I could touch it. I could even almost shift it a bit." He was a historian first, then ran for national office and in his second term was a junior, sometimes rebellious, cabinet minister dealing mainly in foreign affairs. His trouble, when it came to platforms and policies and both international and domestic matters, sounded like an overdose of heart and an eloquent but very impatient desire to accomplish. Lila read about him occasionally in the newspapers. His name, when they met, was familiar.

Sometimes when they watch the news on television, he may still point to some faraway leader. "Poor asshole's way over his head. He thinks he's running things, but you watch, he'll be gone as soon as the guys who put him there make their money and run." And it's often true that eventually the totemic president or prime minister does indeed vanish, sometimes right off the face of the earth.

Lila is impressed, even slightly thrilled, when he predicts these events. Not that she doesn't regret the attendant upheavals and slaughters, but prior, inside knowledge is exhilarating, undeniably.

Tom has admitted to similar feelings, and also to some pleasure in the domestic side of the game. "Figuring out deals and alliances ahead, it's like chess," he has told her, "except now and then you'd be reminded it wasn't chess, and moves had real effects. And then, too, you could watch people forget all their intentions and get wrapped up in tactics and go completely to hell. If nothing else, it was a good lesson in knowing when to stop."

It was not Tom's choice, however, to stop. Voters made that decision for him, and for his party, turfing them both so that he became, in the space of a day of balloting and a night of counting, a historian again.

Although rather a cherished one this time. Rather a triumph, if a minor one, for the university to lure a man with both respectable academic and political credentials. Tom also writes occasional brisk analyses of this trade war and that atrocity for magazines and newspapers, and retains, Lila understands, a credibility, and even glamour, to a few yearning undergraduates. Nevertheless, he remarked recently, sadly, "The past gets remote pretty smartly these days. You have to keep dancing to have much of a future."

This conference is part of the dance, she supposes. So what sort of sacrifice might he really be making to spend almost two weeks instead with her?

They'll rent a car and head off along roads and lanes, exploring and stopping where they feel like it, walking now and again, curling together in strange foreign beds, sitting together in pubs and on seashores. They will build picture after picture of shared views to take home.

She will not—not—think of going home.

He'll have to get little gifts for his wife, and his two grown-up daughters, and his one baby grandson. Lila will wander off on her own for a while then.

Tom's wife, Dorothy, runs a craft supply shop. Lila, hardly a crafty sort, has never set foot in the place, but there's no avoiding seeing people when academic circles collide. They've all turned up, inevitably, at the same necessary receptions, but Lila is careful to move in opposing directions. Tom said his wife, who from a distance looks a pleasant enough woman, started the store, where apparently she sells things like bits of felt, ceramic doodads, balls of yarn cuttable for rugs or rag-doll hair, that sort of thing, when their daughters were in high school and he was in politics.

"She was lonely, and she hated politics. She went into a huge depression for a while. You know that stage; I guess it's common, especially for women." No, Lila does not know that stage; why would he imagine she might? But she nodded.

"Understandable," he went on, "but tough. I had to admire how she pulled herself out of it. I tried to help, but I wasn't much use. Now, sometimes, I hardly know her. She's really intent on what she does. And a pretty good businesswoman, it turns out."

Well. Could anything be more obvious? A drift of attention, a diversion of interests, a discomfiting, bewildering strangeness in the formerly familiar air?

Does it matter that it's obvious? These things happen, life goes on, all that. Some events and shifts are more inscrutable than others, and this just isn't an inscrutable one, that's all.

Good for Tom's wife, Lila thinks. She wouldn't wish her ill. She does imagine a handsome craftsman wandering into the shop one day, in search of yarn or one of those ceramic doodads, and sweeping Tom's wife right off her feet.

Oh, Lila roots for love in whatever form it takes. Including hers and Tom's, of course. She reaches out to squeeze his thigh, and he turns to her and smiles.

Pilots really ought to have voice lessons if, when they switch on their sound systems, they're going to sound high-pitched and quavery. Even speaking the usual altitude-weather-time-of-arrival-hope-you-enjoy-your-flight benediction, this fellow sounds uncertain; as if he's as surprised as a Wright brother to have finally gotten so high in the air.

"Dear me," Lila says, and Tom smiles. After so long, they understand a good deal without words.

Also, even after so long, there's a good deal they don't understand, with or without words. The care, Lila thinks, with which every word should be chosen! And then the care to be sure that it's heard as it's meant. Too exhausting, really, to undertake easily, lightly, without grave commitment.

No wonder there are wars, and back-fence disagreements. It's a challenge, all right.

Still, Lila loves both words and Tom, and never mind the imperfections, limitations. Perfection, anyway, would be onerous—imagine! "I love you," Lila says, and again Tom smiles; as if he knows exactly what she means.

Their flight attendant looks far more confident than the pilot sounds as she goes into her broad pantomime, demonstrating escape routes and techniques to be used in the event of disaster. Her gestures are so extreme they make the odds of disaster infinitesimal and almost absurd. Even so, Lila, however often she flies, never manages not to watch, tracking with her eyes just where oxygen masks would fall from, and where escape lines lead in the aisles, and where the emergency exits are, and just who is sitting there.

Anyway, it seems rude to ignore, as many do, the effort of the performance. Even a bad play deserves some attention; although Tom, bending to fiddle in his briefcase, appears not to agree.

He pulls out one of the conference working papers, but that's all right; he warned her he'd have to spend a little time preparing, and she has a *New Yorker* waiting in her purse beneath the seat ahead. It's a luxury for her not to be carting work around. It's another luxury to have so much time together, she and Tom, that they can spend some of it in separate pursuits, the way real couples can.

Since this is a holiday, she refuses to linger over that thought.

The man in the window seat by the nearest emergency exit looks awfully big from this angle three rows away.

That could be a good thing or a bad one: he might be strong enough to get the door open fast; but he'd be a bulky obstacle if he got in the way.

This is just Lila's mental macramé, an enjoyably chilling pursuit, like watching a cheesy fright film at midnight.

It's surprising such a big man would want a window seat. She would think he'd feel cramped. Even Tom, who's no giant, prefers the aisle so he can stretch his legs. Lila agreeably sits beside him in the middle seat, although she'd prefer the vacant window one. These are the sorts of adjustments and compromises that come naturally after more than five years.

It's sunny up here above the clouds. Exhilarating. "Look," and she nudges him. "It's like a separate universe, isn't it? So detached. A temporary unreality, I always think. A happy respite."

In the classroom she never sounds so disjointed; nor in meetings, nor in conversations with Patsy or Nell. But more and more with Tom, she hears herself lapsing into an odd, worrying, staccato inarticulateness. This may just be what happens when people have been together so long they let their concentration relax, attention loosening like old elastic.

Or it may be, either more or less seriously, a sort of untalent, ungift she is cultivating, like being a reverse alchemist, turning gold thoughts into lead words. She would like to ask him about that, because the idea amuses her and because it might also appeal to him.

In their early days they talked for hours, leaping ahead as if topics were rocks in a river they were trying to cross.

"Yeah," he says. "A happy respite for sure." He touches her hand. So that's okay.

"What are you most looking forward to?"

"You, of course." He is smiling. "Just being with you."

Beyond indulgence, does he know how urgent these days are? Although she can also see hurdles. Planning and packing, she didn't entirely take them into account. Shut up, Lila. She supposes that partly it's nerves. They've been away together before, of course, but never so far for so long. These two weeks are a promise, but also a test.

It's three years since Lila's been to England, that time travelling alone to a conference, a dull but necessary one to do with methods of teaching literary analysis. It was in the north, in Leeds, and just for a week. It's a light kind of feeling, being so distant from regular life, whatever that is: able to look back—of course she missed Tom—but freed of connection.

In that week, she took a rather appealing, passionate man into her bed. This, she considered at the time, had to do with distance, experiment, playfulness, random pleasure. It had to do with her, not with Tom, or for that matter with love, or with faith. The man was forty, a few interesting years younger than Lila. He was at her conference, but his academic interests were not hers, leaning as they did towards certain French philosophies of content and language. She has, she thinks, sufficient grip on these theories, but finds them by and large tedious and unbeautiful.

His ideas—Paul's, his name—were hardly what appealed. What appealed was that he was inventive, and a stranger, and was drawn to her for his own reasons, into which she had no grounds to inquire. He did mention his age often enough that she supposed he might simply be having trouble being forty. She enjoyed his large hands and the sensation of his beard on her skin. She thinks there is sometimes a special generosity, or abandon, with lovers who are mainly strangers: who know they have nothing to sustain.

This sort of event, not unknown in other, previous journeys and conferences, is entirely delicious: all loose ends, free desire. Same for Paul, of course. They both said at the end, each heading towards different homes, his in the south of England where a wife and two young children were doing whatever they did in their lives, that it had been glorious and would be gloriously remembered. They said goodbye with affectionate and grateful smiles.

Is that sort of thing heartless? Lila thinks it's more like going to a good movie, or reading a good book: an event set apart, and if there are effects, they are mainly benevolent, adding scenery, some knowledge, even some depth to a life.

Tom, of course, might not have agreed. "Did you have a good time?" he asked when she returned. "I missed you a lot." They fell into bed. His skin was smooth. She was not nostalgic for beard or lean flesh.

"Tell me all about it," he said. Instead, she told Patsy and Nell. So, after all, it did mean something: a small, flailing last gasp.

She wonders vaguely how Paul is now, and what he's doing, if he still has a beard, if he's still lean, if he still gets all he can out of conferences. Some of his literary theories are falling out of fashion, so he will have to adapt swiftly or become suddenly, sadly old, at least in the academic world.

Dear Tom. She supposes he would think her faithless; although it's not how he sees himself, heading home each night to the crafty Dorothy.

The flight attendant is coming their way with her rolling, clattering cart. She looks to be in her early twenties; about the age of Tom's daughters. "What would you have thought if one of your girls had wanted to do that for a living?" Lila nods towards the young woman whose name, according to the tag on her military-blue bosom, is Sheila. Blue jacket, demure matching blue skirt to the knees, pale yellow blouse—stuffy colours broken by a vivid red scarf at her throat. How many experts met for how many hours to come up with this uniform, with its message of stern dependability, but also a hint of flamboyance?

Lila's own experience of meetings suggests many, many hours indeed.

"The truth?" Tom looks at her seriously. "I'd have been disappointed. Unless it was just for a while, for the sake of travelling or getting some kind of experience of the world. But not as a career." One of his daughters is married, stays home and provided Tom with his grandson; the other's a graduate student in math. "I wouldn't like the idea of them having to serve people like me and smile for a living." He grins. "But I don't expect what I thought would have made a blind bit of difference. They've always done what they want."

Not unlike their father.

"Sir? Something to drink?"

"Scotch and water, please. And one for the lady." Lila snorts—the lady! But Tom's sense of humour can be unpredictable, and briefly he looks wounded. "Sorry. Order what you want. I'll drink your Scotch."

"No, no, it's fine. Just right." She takes a sip, to demonstrate her willingness, benevolence towards him.

But good grief. The day they met, he'd introduced himself at the end of a long and tedious session of the university senate to do mainly with hiring policies. Tom himself, for all she knew, was among the aging, irritable white men intent on their grievances.

"I was watching you," he said. "You obviously feel strongly, but you keep composed, and when you speak, you're calm and to the point. You stopped me from disgracing myself. Honest to God, for a while there I thought I'd have to get up and howl, go running out. What century do those guys think they're living in? Who do you figure they think they are?"

Her surprise must have shown, because he frowned slightly before he grinned. She loves how fast his face can change; and has also, at times, been unnerved. "You made an assumption, didn't you?" he asked. "Well, you're wrong. I earned my job, and I deserve it, and I'm extremely good at it. That's what I wonder about those guys: are they scared they're not good enough to survive a little competition? Screw that."

He'd touched her elbow to get her attention when he introduced himself. He leaned slightly towards her when he spoke, but not so close that he intruded. They said their names as if they didn't know who each other was. They went to the faculty lounge together. Ordering drinks, he said approvingly, "Not a whole lot of women like Scotch. Why is that?"

"Too corporate for most of us, probably. Too much like, oh, getting strapped into pinstripes. We'd really rather sit around in our nightgowns drinking wine and eating chocolate, that's our idea of a good time."

"But not yours?"

"Oh yes, mine too, absolutely. This," and she waved her Scotch, "is just for when there's no chocolate, and a nightgown is out of the question."

Maybe if he'd been wildly attractive, or particularly available, she wouldn't have mentioned nightgowns. Even five years ago, Tom wasn't those things: wildly attractive or, certainly, particularly available. Even then he was slightly balding and slightly pot-bellied. There were lines of laughter and concentration around his eyes and mouth, though; a keenness to his bones, a sharpness to him.

Sometimes Lila has been able to spot an ally or a friend right off the bat. Sometimes a lover, too, but not this time.

"Are you attached?" he asked.

"Not any more."

"Tell me. But let me get us more drinks first."

She was forty-two. She loved a few friends and relatives. Now and then she could be excited by a student or a thought, but she'd spent so long with so many of her colleagues that familiarity had, by and large, with the exception of Patsy and Nell, toppled into disinterest or contempt. She studied and researched, wrote papers and two critical books on her specialty, which is Anglo–North American women's writing in the first half of the twentieth century. People tend to say, "Oh yes, Virginia Woolf," as if that's all there is to it, as if words were never written by Ethel Wilson, or Mary McCarthy, or Sara Jeannette Duncan, or Zora Neale Hurston, or for that matter by Zelda Fitzgerald, not only Scott.

She stood regularly in front of rows of dazed faces, seeking out the ones that might be dazzling. She rolled words and glorious sentences off her tongue, watching to see where they might land.

"'Come and stand in my heart,'" she recited, "'whoever you are, and a whole river would cover your feet and rise higher and take your knees in whirlpools, and draw you down to itself, your whole body, your heart too.'" Once, she also spoke those Eudora words to Tom; telling him something, as well.

She felt in middle age, when they met, not beautiful, she never was that, exactly, but as if she might age well. She considered her history lively and eventful and not, compared with many others, tragic. She couldn't quite tell, looking into mirrors, just how she was changing, or was likely to change, except for grey showing up here and there in her hair. Her eyes, pale blue-grey and large, were her best feature, in her view. They still gave an impression of innocence, but she couldn't count on that continuing. At some point experience would start to show up in the gaze. Or she would come to need glasses.

And then Tom.

"Tell me," he repeated when he'd returned with their drinks. The table was small and round. His hands circled his glass. He had a scattering of brown hair on his knuckles, but nothing excessive. His long fingers looked capable.

"My last lover," she began, "had fat, godawful sausage fingers."

His solemn, attentive expression collapsed.

"No, really," she protested, laughing also. "I could picture myself going into a butcher shop in a big tweedy coat and a flowery scarf, hair up in curlers, carrying a shopping basket and standing at the counter pointing at a tray of Geoff's fingers, saying, 'I'll take those, they should fry up real nice.'"

That, of course, was very near the end.

"My God, you women." Tom was still laughing. "You're cruel."

"Yes," she said. "We can be."

Five years later, she is here on a plane with that laughing man. This still seems to her a kind of miracle.

Lila likes two things about flying. One is that it is virtually a non-experience, merely a bridge between one circumstance and another one, but almost nothing in itself. The other is that just for a little while, her life is out of her hands, and there's not much point in wondering just whose hands it's in, and whether they are nervous or steady or belong to someone she'd like well enough, say, to invite into her home. She is particular about who enters her home.

Naturally she wouldn't like her life to be constantly out of her hands, but these occasions when it must be are relaxing. Almost blissful, in a disconnected sort of way.

"You ever make love in an airplane?" she asks lazily.

She loves the way his lips and the lines around his eyes fly upward. "Nope, never have. You?"

"No, but I'm wondering how it's done. It would have to be in the washroom, wouldn't it, with so many other passengers around? But I understand people do manage."

"Want to try?"

Sometimes they get themselves caught in a whirlpool of challenge neither is willing to be first to abandon; so they have found themselves in some bold and disgraceful positions. Necking in parking lots after late faculty meetings, steaming up the windows of cars, for heaven's sake! It's hard to believe no one has noticed, but that's what they do insist on believing.

"Is that a dare? An invitation?"

Tom looks behind them, a little nervously, Lila thinks. And she thinks also there's relief in his tone when he says, "Oh well, too bad. There's a line-up."

"Damn. Just when I was feeling frisky."

"Wait till tonight. And tomorrow, and the night after that. You'll be a weary old woman by the end of this trip, you'll be rolled back on the plane in a wheelchair."

"And you'll be on a stretcher, smart guy. Wearing splints."

Lila has no idea any more what she would do without him. Her mind goes blank with the thought, and she is a woman whose mind is usually busy with one thing and another. It is terrifying, really, that addiction may have grafted itself to the original fondness and to the consequent, subsequent desire.

No wonder she sometimes flounders, arms and fists churning, trying to get free and creating a little damage in the process. She is horrified by the thought that this might be among the feelings that get called love.

"Christ," she says, stretching. "Couldn't you just die laughing?"

"At us?"

"What else."

Flying in the hands of a stranger isn't scary at all, compared with the two of them.

"My ass is getting sore," he says, also shifting. "Talk to me. Make the hours fly as true and fast as this plane."

"My man of the golden tongue."

"I'll show you that later, too."

Well, who would not grow addicted to a man with lines of laughter and concentration around his eyes and mouth, who says, "Talk to me," and then by and large, more or less, listens? This man who is right now touching his long, light fingers to her thigh, tapping out in code their many happy prospects?

. . . .

two

TOM ISN'T THE ONLY ONE whose ass hurts in these narrow, false-tweed seats. In business class they could both have been stretching out, extending themselves.

Never mind. In just a few hours she'll be able to stretch out every which way.

Lila has learned such patience in the past five years, such restraint—she still is sometimes amazed by her own silences. She could have argued for comfort, after all, could have risked a discussion of the prior and more essential claims on Tom and his resources. Is this another of the disquieting definitions of love? That a person lets little things slide?

Lost things accumulate, binding themselves into large, rock-hard grievances.

She has almost forgotten how it feels to eat fearlessly

in a restaurant with a lover, or stroll openly down a street, or enter a gallery, a movie, a play, without watching out warily. She feels this keenly, although Tom insists he does too. "I don't like it any more than you do," he claims, and she knows that he means it, as far as it goes.

For these two weeks they can eat freely in restaurants, embrace whenever they want, go anywhere at all without looking around. Already they're on an airplane together, it's begun. A little stiffness is nothing.

When this trip is over, will they be able to go back to their old ways?

Her complaints, she knows, would not be met with widespread sympathy.

She catches the occasional talk show, like anyone else, and has witnessed the script for these matters. "We went through a bad patch," a couple will tell television cameras and audiences of millions, about infidelities and tests of trust. "We're working to put it together again. We're getting counselling, we're trying hard."

"I'm so sorry," the straying partner insists, repentant and abject and guilty. "I'm grateful she's willing to give us another chance. I've learned my lesson. I hope she can forgive me, and I can earn back her faith."

A touching tableau. One, Lila always observes, with a character missing.

"Hey, hold on!" she imagines that anonymous, abandoned third figure crying, wagging a finger at the TV screen, reeling from her own betrayal. "What the hell just happened? A minute ago I was a huge, important secret, not to mention the love of his life, and now I'm a penny that fell through his pocket? Wait just a minute here."

Well, there's nothing to do, really, but laugh. Or give up.

"What are you smiling about?" Tom asks.

"Talk to me," he says in warm times; and in sturdy times. "You can tell me anything." Well no, not always.

"I was thinking," Lila says instead, "about what people look for in each other. Like magazine surveys, you know? What do women want in a man, what do men prefer in a woman? Women always say things like humour, kindness, intelligence, tenderness. And probably that he has a decent salary and won't be a burden. What would you say? What would you look for?"

"In a woman?" He pauses, waits a beat, grins. "Enormous breasts and a brain the size of a walnut. That's pretty much it. Why? What do you want in a man?"

"Huge penis. Tiny chick-pea of a brain."

"Ah, Lila." They're laughing. "I love you to death."

"And isn't that just like a man."

There. That's why she loves him. Exactly that: laughter. And intelligence, kindness and tenderness. And his impatience. Also his patience. His salary is not her concern, except when she ends up spending a transatlantic flight in the cheap seats.

And she likes that, in fairness, he cannot say anything like, "Where were you?" or "I don't want you to do that." There is much to be said for this variation of love. Nell's second husband caused trouble that way. "I think," she told Patsy and Lila, "I'm divorcing him just so I can get out to a movie with you guys without a big hassle. Although of course you can't exactly say that to the lawyers."

Here are other pleasing pictures: Tom's intently loving face above hers, her fingers reaching to his cheekbones. He can hover in bed like a whirlybird, so attentive only the two of them and the moment exist.

Is that overwrought? Stylistically excessive and, more seriously, quite unrealistic?

He has most tender eyes, a very dark blue. Even darker when he is ardent or, for that matter, angry.

Playing badminton in her back yard on a windless hot day, both of them taut to win, because they are people who like to win, but laughing also at their own determination. Behaving like children; which may be the point, or at any rate the theme. Tom, sweating, taking off his T-shirt, baring his pot-belly, with its narrow trail of dark hairs, to the light. Men can do that and think nothing of it.

She likes that belly, silhouetted here and there in various circumstances in her memory. It's like an extra warm presence, something more to embrace, and rather endearing. She hopes he feels the same about hers.

Also, really, she adores his penis, his fingers, his tongue. She is entirely happy in his hands, which is not something she can say about all the hands she's been in.

Who knew that at forty-seven her imperfect body would still be turning in clever hands? And that her own hands (Tom says) are clever in return. And (Tom says) her tongue, breasts and other very sensitive parts. Who knew she'd be lucky enough to find, at this advanced stage, such an adept and clever lover?

"Advanced stage" has its piquancy, which perhaps adds zip. There is awareness of bodies changing, winding down, time running out.

"Come on, Lila," Tom says again. "Tell me."

She grins more broadly. "I was thinking how much I like fucking you. How much I'm looking forward to a whole lot more of it."

"Lila! People can hear!" He's laughing too, though. He is tickled, at least when they're safe, by mischief.

Usually, she must be more discreet. "I guess," mock-wistful, "ripping off your trousers to give it a go in public will be as illegal in England as it is at home."

"Only in the streets, where the horses might be frightened. But we may find a deserted moor, who knows, if we look."

"My Heathcliff."

"My Cathy."

Lila's back yard is no deserted moor, but they have made love out there, forgetting, or ignoring, the perils. Well, fresh air and danger—pretty exhilarating, pretty heady. And here's another of his appeals: because he asks, "Remember when we made love in the grass? I'd never done anything quite like that before."

It's a grand thing, having a history that contains so many views and memories, just the two of them. Lila feels greedy for shared visions, possibly because with Tom she feels deprived of them. Heroin to an addict, booze to an alcoholic, chocolate to a child—Lila wants more and more and more.

"I surely do. Stuffy hot night and mosquitoes. I got bites, and grass stains on my butt. Loved it. Just loved it."

"I got the grass stains on my knees. Do you think any of your neighbours saw? I wondered about somebody getting up for a piss and glancing out the window. Made me hope my ass held up okay in moonlight."

"Your ass *is* moonlight. Anyway, they'd more likely have heard us, but they'd be too polite to mention it. And what could they say? 'Next time you're going to have enormous orgasms outside at midnight, could you please keep the noise down, we have jobs and need our sleep'?"

They are giddy with giggling, like children at recess, heads together, talking nonsense.

What did she expect when they started? She guesses she expected herself to be cooler, less involved, less volatile and vulnerable. It may also be that she expected to be more vital to him. She may have imagined she would outweigh everyone else.

As if it were a matter of weights and measures.

As if it were not.

"We'd better shape up," he says. "We'll get kicked off the plane." This makes them laugh more: the picture of being hurled, strapped into parachutes if they're lucky, into the freezing air and down, expelled for misbehaviour.

"I keep wondering how a nice English professor got to be so vulgar." He uses the word "vulgar" as if it's one of those chocolates that splash cherries and cream into the mouth; as if it's delicious. "Was it something you read?"

"Absolutely. That, and a few other pleasures." It is true, stories are not insignificant in a life, wherever they come from. Television also, Lila expects, although more, say, for her students than for herself. But what goes in comes out somehow; nothing is wasted or entirely lost, either to the keen observer or to the porous personality.

This has little to do with vulgarity, but Tom, for instance, might be unnerved to know how alert she is to shifts of his limbs and to his alterations of tone. The alertness he does discern has sometimes annoyed him. She supposes it can make him feel exposed, or burdened. She supposes she might feel that way also, faced with acute attentiveness.

But a smart child, and Lila was a smart child, keeps an eye, which is not a trick that gets unlearned, although it doesn't necessarily get much sharper, either. She can sniff tension and identify camouflaged joy or distress, but that does not particularly help to track causes or ways to repair.

"I learned practically everything I know from stories," she tells him. "Reading them or watching them." He will assume she is referring only to fiction, but she is not.

A child has no way of knowing the origins of adult tensions, but a wise child knows they're there, and when they're dangerous. Not, for Lila, physically dangerous, not like that kind of terrible story, but with a kind of thick-aired, mysteriously grown-up resentment that could make it hard to breathe around the house.

Whatever did this, a single, dramatic, huge event or a series of smaller, unforgivable, unforgettable sins, is beyond Lila, even now. But something between her mother and her father threw a silence like a sheet of glass between them.

It couldn't have been money; her father was in charge of a bank branch's loans and mortgages and certainly earned enough for comfort. Not a woman, women, either: he was too perpetually, when not at work, around the house. A man? Surely not. Not her mother, a woman dedicated to doing good, if not exactly to goodness itself.

Something sexual, then, between the two of them? Something profoundly passionate, at any rate, and secret.

Could Lila have asked? After she became an adult and could have inquired as an adult, would they have answered her?

If they had little to say to each other, they also had little to say about each other. In their different ways, they were ferocious, clasping their shared passionate secret tight to themselves.

Lila and her brother, Don, endured painful dinners during which their father seldom spoke, and their mother chattered about her days, and Don's and Lila's days, her voice so falsely, brightly high that Lila's teeth could ache by the end of a meal.

At night her parents went separately to her room to tuck her in, and then to Don's. Her father leaned down to kiss her forehead; her mother tugged the covers up and gave them a brisk, efficient pat. Then what did they do with the rest of their evenings, with no children between them? Supposing despair, Lila still cannot bear to imagine.

She felt pulled between them like a rope. She felt she and Don held them together like a rope. The children of divorce, she thinks now, too often lack appreciation for their circumstances.

Beginning school, she stared uncomprehendingly at Dick and Jane and their beaming, encouraging parents. From the bookshelf at home, *A Child's Garden of Verses* didn't echo with any vagaries of love she could recognize. Could her parents ever have resembled the Romeo and Juliet of her children's version of Shakespeare? She wondered what would have happened to Romeo and Juliet if they had lived. The bitter secrets of *A Girl of the Limberlost* felt more familiar, and for a while, she was quite at home in the fraught dramas of the Brontës.

She read as if her family were more than the humans involved, but were also a set of stories she wasn't advanced enough to grasp.

Don had his own ways. He stayed out a lot and denied an interest in thick air. Perhaps associating Lila, too, with gloom, he avoided her as well. None of this is a subject he will discuss; or maybe, it occurs to her, it's not one he can bear. He and Lila still don't have much in common except the colour of their eyes, affection for his children, and one terrible event.

He's on his second marriage, though. He must at least have learned not to stick around once something irretrievable has occurred.

It is now Lila's view that her parents went wrong for reasons that do not concern her; that had only to do with adults, not their children. This can happen. There is nothing about marriage, or well-intentioned promises, that prevents it from happening.

It is necessary to be able to get free when it happens.

"You okay?" Tom asks, and Lila realizes she has put a hand to her throat, as if she feels sick, which she doesn't.

She nods. "You?"

"Yeah, but I think I'll hit the john. Or at least the line-up for it."

"Queasy?"

"No, the Scotch. And the excitement. Anticipation. Shit, Lila, you don't know how much I've looked forward to this."

He is such a goddamn sweet man, she could squeeze the life out of him.

How is the atmosphere in his household? Thick with secrets, of which Lila is surely the thickest? Or is it mainly an efficient, time-tabled flurry of two busy, preoccupied people?

Tom keeps secrets in all directions. He has more than the usual quota of privacies.

"You have no faith," he has several times complained. In him, he means. "Trust me," he says, and she does, as best she can.

He will talk freely about his daughters, if not his wife. He speaks of them proudly, and as if they are holy, and as if, even now, he can make them, good or ill, what they will be.

"But," Lila has argued, from the disadvantaged view-point of the childless, "you can't ever tell what's going to go ping in a mind. You have no idea what'll be remembered, or how, or why, for that matter."

"I know," he agreed, "you're right," but his heart wasn't in it.

What Lila meant, though, is that, for instance, no one would have imagined Aunt June would have stuck, somewhat larger than warranted, in Lila's own mind: a woman long dead, who wasn't really an aunt, and who probably wasn't even especially fond of Lila. Has she ever mentioned Aunt June to Tom? She's told him so much, it's hard to keep track.

Each summer of her childhood, her parents and Lila

and Don made the hundred-mile drive to spend a week with her mother's parents. As they turned in the laneway, Lila's grandmother would be stepping from the old brick farmhouse, her hair wrapped in a thin braid around her head, her arms open, her print housedress (whatever happened to housedresses? Same thing that happened to housewives, Lila supposes) protected by an apron, her face flushed from the heat of her kitchen.

Lila flew from the back seat into those arms. Don tore off to the barn and its haymows and kittens and breathtaking sweet-sour smells. Later the two of them would cross paths, switch places, and sometimes they were even together, climbing into trees and haymows, catching frogs, wading in the little river.

Every year, that small summer period was suspended from real time. In that household, people even older than her parents were in charge, and those older people were wholly indulgent, embracing. Lila, off her watchful hook, felt feverish with relief.

The good part about going to see Aunt June, who was actually a neighbour, was that Lila's grandmother would pack a small picnic and they'd head off, the two of them hand in hand together along the path the cattle and farm equipment used through the fields. Her grandmother identified birds, and pointed out groundhog holes, and she and Lila discussed the shapes of clouds and she called to the cattle, who each year frightened Lila for a while, until she got accustomed again to their peaceful, limpid curiosity.

How old was she before she understood they were being fattened up for slaughter? She knows she saw her grandfather slightly differently then.

Lila's grandmother, who smelled of laundry, lilac and yeast, and who had many tones of voice, told her, "Be nice, now. I know June's a little bit different, but she's my very good friend." She was, Lila guesses, her grandmother's version of Patsy, or Nell; who are, as far as Lila knows, the only people in the world aware of where she is now and how she is spending these two weeks.

When June was in her early twenties, a tractor rolled over on her father—"squashed him flat," Lila's grandmother said—and her mother died a few months later. "Broken heart." Was that possible? It sounded terribly romantic.

If Lila's father died, Lila was sure her mother's heart wouldn't break. Her mother's heart seemed more tuned to outside sorrows, and somewhat hardened to her own.

Lila tried to imagine what would happen to herself and Don if either her father or her mother died. How they would feel. Her mind went blank; as, apparently, did June's, more or less. She stayed on alone, on her little patch of land, but since, Lila's grandmother said, she blamed machinery for her father's death, and thus her mother's, she refused, like a Mennonite, to have anything to do with it again. So she never drove a car, and wouldn't have an electric stove. She had an old wood one and cut her own wood for it, because obviously she wouldn't hear of a chainsaw. She grew her own vegetables, and for other supplies she either walked four miles to town and back, or somebody like Lila's grandparents picked things up for her. Naturally there was no vacuum cleaner, and she did all her washing by hand and hung it out on a clothesline.

She must have been very angry. Her father was careless with machinery, her mother didn't love her enough to stay alive, and so, it appeared, June turned her own life ridiculously, fanatically over.

She also raised goats, quite a different and more disagreeable matter than cattle, and when Lila and her grandmother reached June's land, her grandmother

scooted them through the gate, keeping a good grip on
Lila's hand and the picnic basket. "Now, don't show fear,"
she'd say. "They won't bother you if you look bold and
confident." Which Lila considers one of the more useful
lessons she learned from her grandmother, although it
didn't exactly work with the goats, which came racketing
up, butting each other and sniffing and taking little runs
at Lila and her grandmother, who kept saying things like
"Keep moving now, we'll be there in a minute," and
"Shoo," and "Keep back, you nasty thing."

Past June's rickety porch, and the screen door with its
holes and dents, there were—what else?—more goats:
lying in the kitchen; galumphing around the living
room; resting on Aunt June's bed, on top of beautiful,
wrecked old quilts. There'd be a kid or two being bottle-
fed, or a billy cleaning off Aunt June's breakfast plate,
because she just set dishes down on the floor to be
licked. She said she and the goats didn't have anything
they couldn't give each other; which is why Lila's grandmother packed their lunch.

Still, June sold milk and cheese and nobody died from
it. It's true men didn't ask her out to dinner, but they did
buy goats from her and slaughter them, which was the
one thing she wouldn't do herself. Lila's grandmother
said, "June, it really might be easier for you if you didn't
give them names." But she did; the moment one was born
she'd call it something. Lila remembers June introducing
her to one lounging on the bed. "This is Delilah, she's a
lovely little girl just like you. Would you like to pet her?"

Frankly, Lila thought Aunt June herself looked a bit
goatish, scrawny, brown and slightly whiskered. How
could this person be the best friend of her own fastidious
grandmother?

But when the two of them talked, what revelations for
a listening child! Who was getting married, who wasn't,

who was pregnant—"expecting"—and who wasn't, who was fighting or drinking or carrying on.

It's rather sweet that that's what they called it: carrying on.

They had some concept of what they called "decency." From what Lila could tell, they considered it the basic requirement for fixing almost any difficulty, and judged it to have less to do with rules than with tolerance: giving people room. This would have been especially evident to June, who must have known people found her odd. Certainly Lila, off in a corner eating her sandwiches, dodging the goats, thought she was weird.

Lila still suspects June and her grandmother were right, though: that if their version of decency were a first principle, the rest would only be details. Tom, however, when she suggested that once, looked almost insulted. "I expect there's more to politics and history than that, really."

"I wonder. Really. Politics and history are the details, but humane behaviour, respect—that might be the true trick." But it was not a subject to linger over. She and Tom are not necessarily a good pair to discuss decent behaviour. Look at them.

On the other hand, Lila has considerable respect, which is surely at least part of a decent regard, for Tom's wife. She can make the argument (although not with Tom, who's touchy) that Dorothy is a grown-up woman, not a bit helpless, who can see what is there to be seen if she wants, and can make her own choices, as in some respects she already has. She is fully equal to Lila, or Tom, in all this; and more than equal in some ways.

As reasoning goes, that may tip towards the specious. At least it's tortuous; although it's also gratifying, how supple Lila's mind can be. It makes her laugh.

When she and Tom reach England, will they still dodge certain subjects? But from that great distance, certain subjects may not be interesting, or important. The two of them will be very busy with pleasure, using time, building their pictures together.

Lila's grandmother said she would have loved to travel, but she never could. With June, she laid out her troubles the way June set down plates for the goats, which was how Lila heard she was sometimes lonely and not always happy. Once, Lila's grandfather gave her a box of chocolates and she was so touched she was almost in tears telling June. Or for all Lila knew, she was almost in tears for something else. "I'm so tired," she said.

Who else could she say that to but June, who didn't tell her, "Buck up," or "Really, though, you're very lucky." She said, "I know," and "Yes." They were friends. Then, to Lila, this was affection of an unfamiliar kind.

The autumn Lila was ten or eleven, after her family was home from their holiday, June slipped in her yard, cracked her head, knocked herself out and also broke her hip. She lay outside in the rain for more than a day, until a man looking to buy cheese finally found her. She died in the hospital a few days later, of pneumonia.

When her grandmother told Lila this on the telephone, her voice was dry and unsentimental. Lila was startled by death, someone she knew, and sad for her grandmother, truly, but she was too young to have a real notion of how much the event must have mattered. "I'm really sorry, Grandma," she said. Those weren't enough words for the occasion; scrambling for more, she asked, "What happened to the goats?"

There was a pause, and when her grandmother spoke again, her voice had a choking sound that made Lila feel awful. She had said the wrong thing? Or her clumsy sympathy was of no use? "Your grandfather took care of them. They were sold off for slaughter. He's bought up her land, too." He'd have had no more idea than Lila why her grandmother was upset about that, and if he had known, how could he have understood? What he had done, tidying up June's small estate, would have made kind, practical and profitable sense to him.

It did not seem strange to Lila that it was not her grandmother and grandfather who were best friends. What was strange, what she hadn't considered before, was that grown-ups needed best friends, leaned on them, cared for them as best they could, and grieved for them. Her grandmother and June also gave Lila her first notion of women who wear different faces and speak different words when they're together. As Lila, Nell and Patsy do. Probably Lila's grandmother and June had their disagreements, just as Lila, Nell and Patsy do.

Nell's three-so-far marriages have certainly puzzled the other two—what exactly is it she wants?—and Patsy's divorce was a trial for them all. They were both on hand when Lila met Geoff, her last lover before Tom, and listened sympathetically when she left him. She doesn't know quite what they think of Tom. "You know," Patsy told her one Saturday night over drinks, "when it comes down to it, we don't give a shit about him. He seems okay, but you're the one we care about."

"So," Nell threw in, "if he fucks you around, we'll just have to hurt him, real bad." They could all laugh, but in hard and unsafe circumstances, it was still a comfort.

What they tell each other, Lila and Patsy and Nell, is that what they will have, in the end, is each other. "We sound," Patsy said, "like kids swearing a blood oath. Should we cut ourselves and pool our blood?"

Nell snorted. "We're women, for god's sake. We don't have to cut ourselves to get blood."

The three of them began teaching about the same time, Patsy in psychology, Nell and Lila in English. They may have met over common difficulties, being women on an unhelpful campus, and in alliances and little plots; but it was an easy step to fondness, and then to confidences. Like love, there is a chemistry to friendship. None of them would dream of telling all their secrets, they're not ridiculous, but they can tell what they want to.

Which is why Nell and Patsy are the only people who know Lila's here.

If she can't remember telling Tom about June, she knows she told them. About, among other things, June's extreme response to a couple of extreme events, the choice she must have made in favour of huge consequences over ordinary limits. "And you know," Lila said, "it looked like something that could happen so easily. Almost naturally. Do you see what I mean?"

"But," said Nell, "as you say, it's about consequences, isn't it? Risks are easy enough, as long as you can take the results." But Nell is braver than either Patsy or Lila, who has not been inclined towards either her grandmother's housedressy, stoic grace or June's gum-booted eccentricity.

Tom seems unable to grasp properly that parents in general, he specifically, can have no idea of the small random moments, obscure influences, undigested observations that create unexpected, unintended fears and desires and patterns in their children. "I know you're important," Lila would like to say, "but lighten up. Not everything has to do with the benign or passionate intentions of parents."

"I know," he would answer. But his heart would still not be in it.

What would Lila's grandmother think of her now? Would she be disappointed, or disapproving, or would she still love Lila without reserve?

Wouldn't it be nice if love remained pure.

"Sorry I was so long." Tom, slipping back into his seat, startles her. "I got stuck in the aisle behind the flight attendant. She'll be here in a minute. You want another drink?"

Nice of him to ask. "Sure. Scotch again?" To clear her head; return her to here from there, switch her back to present from past. Tom may often feel this, flipping through the scripts of his various lives: matinées as Hamlet, evening performances as Lear. Which lines belong where? Lila can sympathize.

Taking their glasses from Sheila, he asks, "Do you know where we are?" He must mean what they're flying over, not actually where they are, which is inside a narrow, flying, magic silver bullet that is carrying him and Lila towards two weeks of wonders.

Sheila checks her watch. "Just heading out over the ocean, I expect."

Lila wishes he hadn't asked. It makes no sense, but water feels more menacing than land, even though they're thirty thousand feet above anything at all. Still, there are strangely textured, unrecognizable shapes lurking in an ocean, however far below it is. On land, creatures are at least identifiable.

"Good." Tom nods happily; so he doesn't feel what she does. "We're getting there."

"I can't wait." Lila thinks everyone on this plane must be looking towards some special outcome, but she and Tom are particularly blessed in that regard, never mind anything below them, or ahead in two unthinkable weeks.

three

ACROSS THE AISLE A little girl is getting increasingly whiny, a petulant five-year-old version of the trim woman beside her, with their mutually turned-up noses; almond eyes; shining, short, dark, curly hair. Attractive, except for the annoying little voice: "I want to do something. What's there to *do*?"

"Let's read your book," the woman says brightly.

"No. I did that before."

"Then how about a game? How about I Spy? You go first. I spy with my little eye—come on, Susie, you spy something."

"No. I don't *want* to."

Good god, all the way to England? Why do people do this to children? Or more to the point, to themselves? Or most to the point, to other passengers, taking the edge off their communal good mood? Tom makes his own contribution to Lila's irritation. "Poor kid," he murmurs. "It's tough for them, sitting still for so long."

"Yes, I was just thinking how stupid it is, trying to do this sort of thing with them. Annoying."

Tom frowns. "They do have rights, you know."

"Perhaps they'd prefer the right not to spend hours in a little seat, in a little space, with a lot of complete strangers who may not entirely appreciate them." It's not that Lila dislikes children. Really. She loves the ones she knows. It's Tom's automatically sentimental defence of them that gets up her nose. Either he forgets how personally she takes his reverence for families, or recollected fatherhood simply overwhelms him.

Lila does wish she loved not just him, but everything about him; although she's been around far too long to imagine such a thing is possible.

"I want to see out the *window*," the child is demanding.

"Well I'm sorry, we're not sitting by a window, we're sitting here so we can get to the washroom without crawling all over people." Mum's starting to sound just a little frustrated. "Now, please, sit down and be quiet, Susie." It must get exhausting to have someone looking to you all the time not only for entertainment, or love, but also for limits and explanations and rules. How alert you must have to be every moment, keeping on top of what's what. Briefly, Lila feels warmly towards the woman, sympathetic.

But then, without so much as a raised, questioning eyebrow in Lila's direction, Tom leans across the aisle, and her sympathy vanishes. "Excuse me, we have an empty window seat if Susie wants to look out for a while. Not," he smiles at the child, "that there's much to see away up here but," he shifts attention back to her mother, "she's welcome to look. I know how hard it is, keeping kids entertained on a trip." Finally, he turns to

Lila. A little late. "You don't mind, do you?" She doesn't bother to answer. "Come on, kids are fun. You could tell her a story."

Does Lila look like Dr. bloody Seuss?

Still, it's not the child. Once she's scrambled past and is kneeling on the seat, looking out enthralled at the clouds passing under them, she's rather endearing. "We're *high*," she tells Lila, turning towards her, little mouth and brown eyes opened wide with amazement.

"We sure are," Lila agrees.

Tom is right in a way: a child's face is irresistible. The appeal is partly in the way young eyes observe every unfamiliar experience: as awesome and very likely delightful. A way of seeing that could keep all the world fresh.

A parent should be purely loving, purely attentive to this gift of seeing. In many, many respects a parent must not fail, but as far as Lila can tell, must always fail anyway.

In any other pursuit, Lila can bear the prospect of falling short: research papers may go under critical knives, lovers come to grief, some students don't learn. But she doesn't think she could bear a young woman, a daughter, turning on her and crying, "What do you know? What makes you think you can tell me anything now?"

As Lila once turned on her mother, over some disagreement she cannot even remember, although she recalls flinging her arms up, and that she was wearing a long-sleeved white blouse—she can still see the sleeves on those flinging arms, cuffed and buttoned at the wrists.

She was maybe sixteen, seventeen. Her mother's lips got very thin.

The odd moment of curiosity here and there, now and then, about having a child with this man or that, or even a true, temporary desire, can't outweigh the possibility of an unendurable moment of failure.

This is not, of course, wholly truthful. There have been other complicated uncertainties and circumstances, and really it may be, she supposes, that decisions have simply flown by unmade. Now if she did want to change her mind, she could not. What a relief!

No, the problem here isn't at all the beauty of children or the adorable Susie. It's Tom. Does he forget who he's with? Can this be how he is in the parts of his life Lila doesn't see? A man who will decide something, even this kind of small something, inviting Susie to join them, without a nod towards a companion's views and desires?

They still have their surprises, and they're not always happy ones. That must work both ways, of course. But no wonder he got into trouble around the cabinet table, was occasionally labelled a "maverick" when he got his name in the papers. No wonder his wife finally flung up her own arms and opened her craft supply shop.

"Sorry," he whispers. "I know what you're thinking and you're right. Only, I was overcome with compassion for a moment. Won't happen again." How cutting he can so quietly, courteously be.

It's also annoying to know she's being so unreasonable she can hardly not laugh at herself.

The window seat does seem to have made Susie happy. She stares and stares at the sky's enormous, brilliant vacancy. "Is it really hot out there?" she asks Lila. "Are we close to the sun?"

"No, I think it's very cold, because it's a different kind of air up here than when we're on the ground. We're a little bit closer to the sun, I guess, but it's still very, very far away."

"It doesn't look cold, it looks hot. Would you get burned if you sat on a cloud?"

That's a little whimsical for Lila's taste, but still, this is a child. "It does look hot, doesn't it? But you'd be surprised how cold it is. Freezing. Brrr." Lila wraps her arms around herself, pretends to shiver.

"Would I need a blanket?"

"Two, at least."

"That's funny, isn't it?"

Lila nods. "It's a funny surprise when things look one way and turn out to be different, that's for sure."

Susie looks puzzled and turns away, back to the window.

When the first meal finally starts coming around, her mother, strength and patience restored, leans across the aisle and calls to her. "Come on, honey, time to eat." She smiles at Tom and Lila. "Thank you so much. I hope she's not been a bother. It really helps, having a break."

Tom *is* a kind man. His heart practically bleeds for people in need. He cannot, for instance, walk past a panhandler, and once when Lila was with him, he stopped and squatted beside a teenager hunched on the sidewalk, under a blanket, to pet and admire the boy's dog and see, by the way, if he could do something to help. "Get your fucking hands off my dog," the boy warned, which would have deterred Lila, but not Tom, who pulled a fiver from his wallet and put it down beside the boy. "I don't know," he sighed to Lila as they walked away. "I don't understand how that happens, a kid living on the streets and only a dog for love." She'd hugged his arm closer to her body. The same sort of instant, compassionate impulse to fix got him in trouble in politics: his kindness overwhelming obedience to fiscal policies.

There's a difference between kindness and gentleness. Lila would say she is more gentle than he, but nowhere nearly as kind. Who knows how many people he will set out to rescue, from boredom or doom, in the next couple of weeks? Lila might catch kindness from him, with a sufficiently prolonged exposure. She might go home good, even saintly.

In that case, goodbye Tom.

Elbows collide as they deal with their dinner, relatively recognizable as a mixed vegetable rice, a salad that does not involve iceberg lettuce and meat that is evidently beef. There's a tiny roll, and for dessert a dish of unsweetened fruit. This is truly a romantic meal; far more so than delicately designed dishes in a small, darkened restaurant, with champagne and candles. Because here they are, side by side in their cramped hard seats, dodging each other's elbows, struggling with elfin cutlery, flying together—imagine!

And in a way, it's as private as any dark restaurant. Individuals get lost in crowds. Here are dozens and dozens of people jammed into this cabin, in which every morsel of space is designed for a purpose and nothing is wasted or useless; but push people together and they are quick to build walls, and Lila and Tom can be quite alone.

All these strangers sitting in their obedient rows are headed in the same direction, but must have utterly varying purposes and sentiments, hopes and desires. Each is a story as well as a person. Lila and Tom, the two of them, are a story; very likely they are also two stories. He has his own, no doubt somewhat different from hers.

Naturally she finds their story compelling, but others' must be interesting too.

"Do you find yourself wondering why everyone's here?" she asks.

"You mean cosmically? The purpose of humanity? Or only why we're all on this plane?" He enjoys teasing her.

"Start small. On the plane."

"I guess I *could* wonder. Or you could just tell me what you think." He also enjoys her telling him stories; says he likes the compactness of fictions, which he considers tidier and rounder than history's messy, straggling facts. A misconception, in Lila's view, but no doubt she equally fails to grasp some aspects of his sense of history.

"Okay," she begins. "Susie and her mother, for instance—I'm thinking you'd need a powerful incentive to load a five-year-old onto a plane for this sort of journey. So how about if the mother's abducting Susie?"

"Why the hell would she do that?"

"Because, let's see, when she's very young, she meets a rich older guy with a lot of power and connections and glamour, and she's dazzled. He's charming and protective, and she thinks he'll look after her. But once they're married, it turns out he's a power freak, won't let her go anywhere or do anything, starts handing out black eyes and bruises. Then they have Susie, but instead of making him better, he gets worse, punching her, once even breaking her arm. He's rough with Susie, too, and she starts worrying about him harming her, and that's too much, that's the end. She can't let him hurt her child.

"But where can she go? On her own she doesn't have anything, or any skills. Still, one day she packs up a few things and sneaks out with Susie, rents a room, finds a lawyer."

"Where does she get the money for that?"

"Oh, from an old high school friend she's managed to stay in touch with, and her brother and sister give her some. Enough. Then she gets a part-time job waitressing, while her sister looks after Susie. She's almost starting to think she can get on her feet.

"Finally her husband says okay, she can have a divorce, but not Susie. He wants Susie. Her lawyer says her husband might well win custody, since he's guaranteeing a good education and all kinds of luxuries, and she can't. So what can she do? She's desperate. She gets all her courage together and tells her husband she'll accuse him of abusing Susie if it comes down to it.

"Even when he was beating her, she's never seen him so furious. He turns very cold. He says if she makes a move against him, he'll kill both her and Susie. That one way or another, she won't keep Susie. The way he's looking at her, she believes him."

Tom shakes his head. "What a mind you have, Lila."

"Well, it happens, right?"

He nods, pushes his tray away, folds his hands across his belly, closes his eyes. He knows, after all, that this is only a story. "Then what?"

"She can only think of one thing to do. She has to get away, run, hide, save Susie. She borrows more money, no idea how she'll ever pay it back, and here they are. She doesn't know what she'll do or where they'll go once they're in England. They might be on the run through Europe for years. Till Susie's a grown-up. But she'll do anything, make any sacrifice, to keep Susie safe. She's already afraid her husband has detectives on her tail and she won't get farther than Heathrow, but she has to give it a shot." Lila takes a deep breath.

"There. The end."

Tom applauds. "Very good."

"Thank you."

It had holes, though, and flaws, Lila knows; not least of them that Susie's mother looks much too relaxed to be a fugitive woman flying from danger into a furtive and desperate future.

"Keep going," Tom says. "Tell me more."

"All right." She looks around. "How about the big guy by the emergency exit, did you notice him?" Tom opens his eyes briefly, stretches to look, nods.

"Say he murdered his wife last night."

Tom's eyes flare open again. "What?"

"Really. Beat her to death, broke all her bones, or stabbed her, or shot her, or put poison in her soup or her after-dinner drink. Then he threw a few things together and bolted, and now he's trying to escape, like Susie and her mother, except for different reasons. He's hoping nobody's found the body yet, and he has a few hours of lead time before anybody starts hunting him."

"Why would he do that?"

Why indeed? Lila can hardly suggest he was having an affair and decided to cut loose (imagine Tom slaughtering Dorothy for such a reason—oh, not funny). "Maybe, let's see, she told him their children aren't really his? Or that he's getting too fat, or drinks too much, or that she hates how he dresses, or the sounds he makes chewing? Maybe she told him she couldn't stand a single thing about him any more."

"And he killed her to put her out of her misery?"

"Something like that."

Those things happen, too.

"He's big," Tom says, regarding the man, "but he doesn't look dangerous. What made you suspicious? Or is this just your day for bad, vicious men? How about if the poor guy is only off to sell, I don't know, shady investments or swampland to unsuspecting Brits?"

"Heavens, no, that's far too dull. Of course he doesn't look dangerous, but that's the point. You know, nine out of ten people who look perfectly ordinary are hiding something dreadful. I believe there are studies to show that."

"No doubt." Tom laughs. He hates how many studies there are proving this, proving that, proving whatever is desired.

"Also, look where he's sitting. Maybe he figures if he slumps in a window seat, he won't be noticeable if anyone's on the lookout for him, but actually he sticks out, he's obviously inexperienced. A man his size used to fly-ing would never choose an inside seat."

"Good point, Sherlock."

"Ms. Marple, please. Anyway, keep your eyes open at Heathrow. Scotland Yard is bound to be on tap for one thing or another."

That also happens. The difficulty is finding stories that do not happen. New, unlikely, unreasonable stories.

"Shouldn't the movie be starting?"

"You'd think so. Going to watch it?"

It stars a man whose talents they both admire. From reviews, they gather it has little resemblance to old-fashioned Westerns, with their white hats and black hats, the clear good and bad which, Lila assumes, must have appealed to some people sometime. Modern moral ambi-guity, she and Tom agree, is more compelling and far more realistic.

Well, naturally they agree on that. Of course they must. Moral ambiguity is practically their motto. They could wear matching sweatshirts with those words stitched front and back.

Most good stories are considerably more ambiguous than the ones Lila's been telling Tom. Everyone has their own perspectives, their own tales, their own points of view, and the question is only whether they're told or not, taken into account or not. If Lila's stories were true, Susie's father would surely have something to say for himself, and so would the man in the window seat. Not to mention his wife. Lila and Tom run into this them-selves: an event she sees one way, he views quite an-other. They may agree both ways are reasonable, but that doesn't mean the differences aren't irreconcilable, and still sometimes startling.

Just a few weeks ago she discovered, for instance, that what she has regarded as lively discussions, he has sometimes viewed as arguments. Imagine how easily one could go years, decades, lives, without knowing that sort of thing—the prospects for misunderstanding are enormous.

What were they talking about? Massacres, that's it, because they were on her sofa having an after-work drink, as they do, and watching the news on television, as they do, and there was some hideous, bloody, senseless outbreak of slashing ill will by one indistinguishable group against another indistinguishable group, sending many limbs flying, much blood spurting, many corpses lying about in dusty roads and ditches. No one on the TV news pinpointed what, exactly, had launched this, but several people sounded certain it would lead to much more and much worse.

Wasn't it astonishing that these people who were now slaughtering each other had, for a fairly long time, been living peaceably as neighbours, as communities, sometimes even as families? Lila thought it was. She wondered what stories, frequently terrible but not always, must lie behind all this.

Surely Tom, the former politician and current historian, would have an enlightening perspective. History as he describes it is mainly a narrative of conflict; rather like news, although he doesn't like the comparison, having been burned on occasion and feeling as he does that news is fleeting and uninformed, and very likely to turn out to have been inaccurate, and certainly lacking in the long view. Whereas history is precisely the long view.

"How do you think a thing like that happens?" she asked. "Can you imagine doing those things? Hacking your neighbours to pieces? And little children? Well, look at that, little children on both sides, hacking and being hacked. Whatever will happen to them? How could their hearts ever recover? Would we be capable as well? I bet we could. I bet it's right beneath everyone's surface. What do you think brings it out?"

He frowned slightly and began to speak of arbitrary imperialism, colonialism, rough boundaries that failed to take inhabitants into account. "It happened everywhere. Africa, Europe, especially Eastern Europe, here and there in South America, even in North America, to a degree. There are always ancient tensions and rivalries, and we probably can't begin to understand them now." He shrugged. "Probably those people can't either, any more. Now it's perpetual revenge, back and forth. In the bones. Or the blood. I don't know."

This was puzzling. What was the point of pursuing politics or history if he could only shrug and regard some matters as hopeless? Anyway, it wasn't quite what she'd been asking.

"I realize," she said carefully, "all that. But what I was wondering, is there something in everyone's bones and blood? Whatever the history, is there something vicious inside humans, and it only takes a scratch on the skin of civility for it to splash out?" Because for all her own relatively peaceful, unviolent life, this is Lila's suspicion.

"Oh, Lila." He sighed. "I don't know. It's been a tough day. Let's not argue about it. You ready for another drink?"

What a surprise.

Mightn't it be interesting to track back their words together and compare how they each meant and heard them? Tom would call that pathological; not in the mad sense (although maybe that, too) but in the morgue-laboratory way of close, intent analysis and scrutiny.

In her work, dissecting texts and stories, Lila's intention is not to ruin, not to be left staring hopelessly at a heap of unreplaceable parts. It's to see the whole more clearly, with an eye to its complexity. To see how even entirely unfamiliar emotions can be felt, and unlikely circumstances experienced.

To have many more lives than her own, and make them, however briefly, imaginable and touchable.

Naturally she and Tom have some different opinions and perspectives, but shouldn't differences be opportunities? Shouldn't they make the two of them bigger, at least prevent them from shrinking? One of the hazards of a safe middle age is the lure of getting little. Lila imagines it gets easier and easier to curl up like old lettuce, turn brown at the edges and wilt into decrepitude. She does not care for that idea at all.

She glances towards him, and sees that he has evidently lost interest and now, for heaven's sake, has fallen asleep—does she have to go on making up stories to keep him awake? And how can he be tired when their journey has barely begun? Some exhaustion from his other life, perhaps, that Lila has no way of knowing about. She has very little idea how his private hours away from her are spent. Perhaps he's had large, unspeakable events on his calendar.

It's rather nice, though, and trusting, the way his head tilts towards her.

Usually when Lila goes to Europe, it's on a flight leaving at night, heading into the sunrise. This is different, flying into the dark. People lulled by a plane's sturdy, tedious sound and the immobility of waiting may fall asleep, like Tom; but won't they be disoriented when they get where they're going?

It's possible he's dozing for no other reason than to store energy for their time together. When he told her once that busy people should be able to grab quick naps whenever they can, she was reminded of something she'd read about the Queen: "Her Majesty never passes up a discreet opportunity to use facilities"; which must account for why she is never caught going knock-kneed about her public chores. "You sleep," Lila told Tom, "the way the Queen pees."

"No doubt I'd agree, if I knew what it meant. A regal sort of compliment, is it?"

Tom met the Queen on one of his overseas political jaunts. "Well, not to say met her exactly, not the way I met you, for instance."

"I should hope not."

"More that I was actually present with a thousand or two other suitably impressed people on palace grounds when she drifted very close by. It's possible she might not recall the occasion."

"Oh, I'm sure she does. Who could forget you?"

"Could you?"

"No, not ever." Which of course, however their story goes, must be true (unless she comes down with one of those forgetting diseases). What isn't exactly clear is just what would be remembered, and how.

I want, she thinks. "Want" is a verb that requires an object, but she can't find the word.

Well, she wants Tom, whose head is nodding closer and closer to her shoulder.

This, she thinks, is how it feels being with him: as if roots have shifted and nudged deeper and deeper, coiling and pushing until they have tendrils in every limb, organ and vein. Important parts of her have come to feel held together by these roots; like shallow land at risk of losing its topsoil if it isn't protected by growth.

Oh dear, another image gone over the top—she keeps, in her enthusiasm, going too far. She shakes her head.

Coming awake with her movement, Tom shakes his head, also. "My ears feel strange. Think there's something funny about the pressure?"

She shrugs. "It never quite suits me on a plane. That

and the air. I always get some awful combination of dried out and puffed up, if a flight's any length at all."

He laughs. "Sounds attractive. You must be a treat by the end." He looks at his watch. "Sorry for tuning out. It wasn't you, it's just that after a while planes always send me unconscious." She didn't know that about him; a good thing to find out, that his doze wasn't personal. And what will he learn about her in these two weeks? Not everything, for either of them, will be pleasing or virtuous, and thank goodness for that.

Now a couple of kids from heaven knows what part of the plane are running up and down the aisle. Susie is watching them, looking shy but willing. Lila hopes shy overcomes willing, because two youngsters playing some antagonistic game this close are already too many.

Adults are also stirring, cramped muscles kicking up trouble. Some people stand and stretch, creating a cabin-wide rustling of cloth that sounds, over the rhythm of engines, like a great flurry of moths' wings.

Somewhere towards the front, a baby is starting to howl.

Tom raises his eyebrows. "Still no movie?"

Lila shrugs again. "Not yet."

"I could use another drink. How about you?"

"Sure. Whenever. She should be around again soon."

He twists to peer down the aisle, turns back, frowning. "There's a bunch of them in the galley, just talking, it looks like. Four of them."

Kind, tender-hearted Tom, and this surprised Lila in their early days, balks at casual service in restaurants and stores. He has been known to toss items he intended to buy on a counter and stalk out if he hasn't been able to get help fast enough, and he can be snappish in restaurants if he thinks the service is not properly attentive. By and large, when they're together he saves Lila the trouble of saying similar crisp words, or making similar crisp gestures herself.

And by and large, that's something to be careful about. She can't afford to start assuming, or depending; falling into roles, like husbands, like wives: men who automatically drive, women who automatically don't drive. That kind of thing. It can get too easy; like letting him order her drink for her.

"Listen," he says more urgently. "Hear that?"

His face has the strangest expression. Unfamiliar, almost scary. What the hell is it?

He is looking beyond her, over her shoulder. His eyes are huge, his mouth hangs open.

"Oh, Jesus," he says softly, with something like awe. "Oh, sweet Jesus Christ."

. . . .

four

OH JESUS, INDEED, OH
sweet Jesus Christ.

Lila doesn't believe it. Then she almost laughs out
loud—imagine even for an instant that her belief or disbelief makes any difference. Imagine a giggle bubbling up
at a moment like this.

She is staring, gape-mouthed, at Tom, who is still staring past her, past the empty seat, out the window. How
can he?

She has already turned and looked, and turned back to
him, just as fast as she could.

That's fire out there. Fire and space; something terribly
present and equally terribly empty.

No.

No, these things happen, but not really. On the news,
yes, or in movies, but not to Lila. It's only—what?—a

scene. She thinks, No wonder they don't show airplane disaster movies on airplanes, and another giggle bubbles up. They probably don't sell airplane disaster books in airport bookstores, either.

Tom's gaze remains locked on the flame-licked wing. He must have a different way of disbelieving than she does. Although fire dances in front of her anyway, between her face and his. She is watching his eyes through a flaring red curtain.

Lila prays for a suspension of event, right now. For anything but the heart-clamping terror against which she is instantly constructing this false, unsteady barricade. She is surprised to find herself praying. Or pleading, actually, the extent of her eloquence reduced to, "Oh please," not even addressed anywhere in particular. Like a scared child: too few words, and too small ones, for very large events.

But it was just a little bit of fire, wasn't it? More hinting than real?

Airplanes must be built with this sort of possibility in mind, there must be mechanisms and manoeuvres. Well, what? Do the people flying this thing, who understand its mechanisms and manoeuvres, even know they have a problem yet?

She and Tom haven't said a word except for his exclamation, although maybe he gasped at first sight, Lila doesn't recall, but knowledge is spreading around them, rippling from seat to seat, row to row, until there's a rising, rumbling tone of horror. Some shouting. Shrieks here and there.

Some kinds of knowledge are explosive, too big to contain. That may be why hands fly up to faces, covering ears, covering eyes: trying to prevent minds from collapsing in on themselves with this new understanding.

Shared terror is far too real, multiplying itself automatically and uncontrollably in some wild formula maybe

Tom's younger, clever mathematical daughter could explain.

Lila's grandmother, telling June of some upheaval, had words for this feeling: "I'm all turned inside out," she'd say, hands fluttering in distress like butterflies.

Tenderly, tentatively, Lila reaches a hand to the side of Tom's jaw, feeling bone. Gristle under the skin.

She can't quite feel her own skin, though. An awful, high scream rises from somewhere behind them, and Lila admires how alert that woman must be, absorbing the impact of disaster so swiftly she can scream like that.

People are starting to move, some trying to run. Some, scattering possessions and wits, are even climbing over seats—where do they think they are going? What do they suppose they are doing? "Be still," she wants to shout. "Everybody, shut up, please, till I can understand this." She can't say just what "this" is. If she could say, would that fix it, or cause it to vanish? Is her faith in words so great she believes the right one could repair?

She hopes the members of the crew are not so foolish. Of course they're not; naturally their faith will be in machinery, not words.

Lila's touch has finally reached Tom, so that his gaze shifts, it seems reluctantly, to her. "Lila?" She can't hear him, but sees his mouth forming her name. "Lila?"

"I don't know." She can't tell if he can hear her. "I don't know," which is no answer, but then, it wasn't truly a question.

There isn't time to say everything twice like that. There isn't time, for that matter, to say everything once.

Maybe she was wrong. Maybe everyone's wrong. She only glanced for a second. On planes, sometimes things look wrong, or reflect in the air strangely, when nothing's really the matter at all. On night flights, sparks in the darkness have startled her on occasion. Maybe these are only sparks in the light.

She turns to look again. Those are not sparks. Those are flickers of flame at the edge of the wing.

Where is fuel stored on an airplane? How could there possibly be fire out there, where the air, as she tried to tell Susie, is so intensely cold? Why isn't someone *doing* something? There must be things to be done. She hopes the crew hasn't been stricken immobile by a disbelief similar to her own.

She turns back urgently to Tom. "This isn't happening, is it?" Surely he could alter reality. He has altered aspects of her reality for as long as she has known him, why not now?

"Oh Christ," he says. "We're going to die."

What?

She could shake and shake him. She's had such hopes, and he's not even trying. If he cultivated a disbelief like hers, could they not, with their combined wills, make this not be happening? Instead, such despair is in his face, along with terror.

She reaches out again to touch his skin. At the moment, she loves and pities him to death, and it does not feel like an odd combination.

Wait. Just wait. She is a rational person, and it's important to know things. With facts, a person can figure out how to feel, but they are flying at the moment without critical information. Not fair.

The running children have disappeared from the aisles. Susie is wrapped in her mother's arms, weeping. Does she understand, or is she just upset by an explosion of adult hysteria? Nobody understands; how could Susie? Why doesn't somebody tell them what's wrong? There might be hope, and no great problem, and nobody's telling them that, either. She starts to stand, to look around, to demand something from someone. She feels Tom's hand on her arm and looks down. "Lila," he says. "Lila, please."

Those words. She is so very weary of hearing them on important occasions. There was a time, early on, when she wanted her and Tom to be together, but "Lila, please," he said.

She said, "Other people do it all the time."

"Lila, please, we can't talk about this. I know they're almost grown, but the girls would be devastated. They're close to their mother, and I don't want to lose them. Maybe it'll be different once they're out on their own."

Which they now are, but even then, Lila doubted it. She foresaw family events rolling into the future—graduations, weddings, births of grandchildren—in a festive parallel universe, followed by various crises, disintegrations, disasters and deaths. All the this and that, forbidding a move. And she was right.

Now this. She has an impulse to say, "I hope you're happy now."

She still can't hear small sounds, like his voice, very well, although shouting and screaming from elsewhere feel as if they're drilling holes in her head.

Prayers used to be promises, bargains: "If I get a doll for Christmas, I promise I'll always be good." Or "If I get a good mark on this test," or "If I get asked to that party"— and always, in return, the promise she'd be good. She guesses she never kept it very well; but she would now. "I'll give up anything, I'll do anything. I'll be so good in my life, if I can only, please, have my life."

Tom is her only really outstanding sin—old-fashioned, unfamiliar word that even at this terrible, bargaining moment doesn't feel like the right one. Without him, she would be lonely and sad, but alive. And she is not young any more, and at least she would remember love, and there must be other pleasures: wisdom, meekness, generosity, all those virtues she seems to have put off acquiring. She isn't stupid; she could probably get the hang of goodness.

"Lila!" His voice now is sharp, and she can hear him quite sharply. "Settle down, Lila. Come on, now, sit down." She realizes she is still standing and that Tom, looking up at her, seems worried. Or disappointed. Or irritable. She can't always tell the difference. Sometimes there isn't much difference. Disappointments and worries irritate him, as a rule; cause and effect blurring together.

"Yes," she says, "okay," and obediently sits.

He keeps a grip, not tight, on her arm. "Keep calm. We need to be calm." He should speak only for himself. He has not earned the full-hearted place in her life that would allow him to speak for her.

Her skin marks easily. There are already flushes of blood around the white marks where his fingers grasped her arm. And her bones are thin. As it turns out, there's not much to her. Tiny freckles on the backs of her hands would sizzle in flames; her bones would collapse at the slightest downward spiral, shatter at a touch of land.

Or, she remembers, ocean.

This is the sort of circumstance in which the deft, sausage-fingered, life-saving Geoff might have come in handy.

Or, more likely, he'd do well in the aftermath, stitching together the uncountable bits and pieces that may fall from the sky.

Poor Geoff, perhaps she was unfair. Perhaps she is also unfair to Tom, and to other people along the line, and to herself, as well.

Don't think and don't look. Keep the mind in the air.

On Geoff, connected as he is anyway with life converted from death. Six years she spent with him, slightly longer than she has so far been with Tom.

The night of her thirty-fifth birthday, Nell and Patsy took her to a restaurant to celebrate. He was at the next table with friends, or more likely colleagues. There was much laughter and drinking of champagne, and the two tables ended up together. Geoff sent her a half dozen white roses the next morning—"A day late, but it should never be too late" the card said, somewhat cryptically, somewhat enticingly.

"I've had some awkward moments," he confided a few nights later over dinner, "since my divorce. Sometimes I've learned that a woman has gone out with me because of my work. I mean, because I'm fairly well known, I guess."

"Yes," Lila agreed, "I expect that can be a hazard."

Down the road there were further words, in other tones. "For god's sake, Lila, you knew from the start how busy I am." Quite true. He went to some pains to tell her his marriage, for one thing, had failed precisely because he was a busy man, and not only that, busy in such a virtuous and necessary way that there was no point in merely personal complaints.

Who would, could, reasonably expect his presence when on the other side of the scale a life was in the balance? Geoff's skilful, pudgy fingers were needed, absolutely needed, to dig beyond flesh into organs and arteries, pulling them out, turning them over, replacing them, sewing bodies together maybe moments from death.

A woman could hardly say to such a man, "Yes, I know the guy has only one kidney and it's disintegrating as we speak, but I've had a really bad week and I'd like to rest on your shoulder, if you wouldn't mind." On the other hand, who unfailingly agreed that, always, it would be more urgent to give pleading speeches to Rotarians than to comfort someone who'd had a bad week?

"I have to," he said. "It's important."

"So are some other things. You should know that. I hope you do."

He said he didn't like her tone; that it sounded threatening. "Up to you"—she shrugged—"what you hear."

She read accounts of his speeches in the newspaper (how well publicized, for one reason and another, some of her lovers have been). "It's difficult," he told audiences wherever he could grab them, "for a physician to ask a grieving family to make such a wrenching decision. But to offer a chance of life—as physicians we must give families that opportunity. It's a greater memorial to the values and spirits of loved ones than the grandest grave-stone, or the most eloquent epitaph." Didn't he sound fine! Didn't he give the most eloquent speeches, himself!

There will be no salvageable organs if this plane goes down, nothing useful for surgeons to "harvest," as Geoff used to put it. Lila found the expression chilling; but it was nothing compared with this bone-clattering cold.

"I'm sorry, sweetheart," Geoff said when Lila's mother died, folding large pink freckled arms around her. "I wish I could be with you." A keynote speech he was giving, at a national conference. He had to fly west, she had to drive east. "I'll call you when we both get where we're going."

Lila's mother died, climbing into bed for the night, from a ferocious attack from her heart. She was only sixty-four, so it came as a shock. Like Aunt June, she lay dying and dead for more than a day before she was found by a neighbour. The despair, picturing those last hours—Lila surprised herself with sounds she'd never heard her-self make before.

But Geoff, with his higher purposes, flew off; and Lila, not unreasonably, began developing a horror of dying alone and going undiscovered.

It appears she may have frightened herself with the wrong pictures entirely. She may die in quite the opposite fashion: in a great crowd, very publicly.

Several times driving back to the town where she grew up, where her stomach knotted and her head developed unaccountable aches when she visited, to which she'd driven eight years earlier for her father's funeral—several times Lila had to pull to the side of the road to weep. Tears broke down roughly half for her mother, half for herself.

Later she thought, tuning out the minister's rambling, beaming eulogy at the funeral, by which time she'd become much calmer, more removed, that probably her mother had finally burst from compressing too strenuously her true thoughts and emotions. "Dead of repression" crossed Lila's mind as an epitaph. She heard herself laugh, quickly covered the sound with a cough. Even a sob; she wasn't proud at that point.

Sheila the flight attendant rushes past, fighting her way to the front past harsh frightened voices and flailing limbs, not stopping for anyone. Her blouse is untucked at one side, her dark hair is no longer quite smooth. Seeing her eyes might tell them something: whether she is scared and doomed, or only determined to get someplace.

She is past before Lila can get a glimpse of her eyes. Anyway, people both show and conceal feelings in different ways, and unless Sheila is actually panicking, it would be hard to define her emotions on such flimsy acquaintance.

If there is a good time for either repressing or concealing rampant emotion, this must be it.

Still, Lila can't believe that things like this happen. People like her don't die; not this way. They die the way her mother did: plainly and privately.

Lila and Don and his recent second wife, Anne, saw the family lawyer, chose and sorted possessions, arranged to put the house up for sale. Don took the television set and the dining-room furniture. Lila took the pink-and-gold-flower-rimmed china her grandmother had passed on to her mother. "That's all you want?" Don asked.

"I think so." Certainly not the embroidery hoops with which her mother stitched pillowcases for the poor or newly married, or the wicker baskets she packed with soups, breads and casseroles for the sick, bereaved or hungry.

An astonishing number of people turned up for the funeral. "She was always so kind," people said, touching Don's black elbow, embracing Lila's black shoulders. "She was a very good woman, your mother."

And so she was. Lila, who has not followed her example, will have many fewer people, with many fewer benevolent memories, at her own funeral. Which may be dreadfully, surprisingly soon. Oh please, she thinks again. I'll do better. I'll be better.

Back home, when Geoff asked about the funeral and its attendant events and characters, she found herself looking at his hands resting with apparent concern on hers. "It's too late and too little, just to describe it," she said. "Too many feelings in a short time. I think it's like a bad joke—you had to be there."

She thought, Those stumpy, porky fingers, I've had them on my body, how could I? And think where else they've been.

There are moments when the eye, or something, is caught, turns over, and everything changes.

"Geoff," she began carefully, "I know you save lives, and have a lot of demands and a lot of people wanting your attention." She wondered what the word was for his expression—preening, she thought finally. He found this flattering, and looked like a plumpish, proud—oh, she didn't know quite what, but some creature that preened. Not a parrot, exactly; a parrot's features were sharp.

"And that's very nice for you, and well deserved, but it's not, as it turns out, very compatible with love. Or with care, for that matter."

She thought that was clear, but apparently not.

"What are you saying? I don't understand what you're talking about."

"I'm saying it isn't a matter of fault, but I'm tired, my mother's dead, I have no more room for generosity, or even understanding, and I'm done."

"With us?" He still wasn't getting it. "With me?"

"You sound astonished."

"But no warning? That's not fair. To come out of the blue, springing this on me."

"Oh, Geoff, there's been plenty of warning. You just haven't heard it." He had many virtues, not all of them public ones: energy, focus, desire, intensity. And love, he said. But he had also been deaf, it turned out.

"Lila, be reasonable! I thought you were better than that. This is what I went through with my wife, for god's sake. I never expected to go through it with you." His finest shot, a comparison with the odious, frivolous, uncomprehending wife.

At least Tom has never done that. Rather the reverse, in fact, and just as upsetting.

"I've done the best I could," Geoff said, and no doubt from his perspective he had. He looked as if he wanted to shake her, or strike her. Had he ever hit his long-gone wife with those ham fists?

He is still giving speeches and doing good work. She still reads his name in the papers, his story continues. Just over a year later—a pleasant, unstrenuous period Lila spent mainly teaching, reading, researching, and playing with Patsy and Nell, going to movies and plays and bars, telling secrets and sorrows and jokes—she met Tom, another good man with much of his attention elsewhere.

These percentages and decimals and tiny increments of love are hard to calculate. Hard, as in both difficult and wrenching. Lila has certainly had much delight from the ways words wander off in different directions.

How do some people stick in one life when even a word can have so many existences? Lila expects that, absorbed in stories of various real and fictional sorts, she has fallen easily into the idea of alteration and flux: that a multiplicity of characters in a multiplicity of situations must have a multiplicity of responses.

That makes today especially unpredictable and volatile. Except for Tom, these are strangers, and at that, who knows about him? Or herself? There's no real telling what the two of them contain, never mind anyone else.

How long has she managed to avoid pictures of what's happening and how they are doing? It feels like forever. If it's even been quite a while, that must be a good, hopeful sign. But it may be a matter of seconds. The mind flies in a crisis. Is time flying?

Is the plane? Well, she does have to laugh.

And again that offends Tom, although she can't see why, it's not aimed at him. "Lila!" His voice slices through the buzzing and din. His fingers, shockingly, burn on her face. "Stop it! You mustn't."

She stares at him, surprised not by pain, but because she never dreamed Tom had it in him to strike her. One way or another, sometimes deliberately, generally not, he has now and then caused her grief, but she has never had a moment of fear he would turn on her that way. Stupid, surely, to start now. How could he imagine frightening her, or punishing her? What does he suppose he could do?

"I'm sorry, Lila, but we have to keep our heads." What

on earth for, when they may lose everything else? She keeps that tiny joke inside.

What's wrong with her? Because he's right, this is awful, not funny. "What's the matter with you?" he asks, and it's a very good question, as well as an amazingly stupid one.

"I'm just not very good at reality, I guess." It's hard to keep her eyes from dancing. Her grandmother used to say, telling Aunt June some event, "I don't know whether to laugh or cry."

Lila is tempted to tell him, "Really, it's one of my gifts, not facing facts very well, and aren't you lucky." Nobody good with facts, for heaven's sake, would spend precious time with a person with firm attachments elsewhere. Only someone with barely an acquaintance with reality would tempt fate with a two-week trip to another country with such a person. What does he think?

One thing she does know something about is fate. She teaches whole lectures on it, as it unfolds in various stories and plays, here and there, over time. She can point to many examples, beautiful words for fate's sad victims.

No doubt the concept runs contrary to the views of a historian. And for a politician, hope, not fate, must be the carrot dangling just ahead.

One thing about fate is that it's a very grand concept. A huge idea to fit oversized characters. Far too big to apply to someone like her. Or to Tom, for that matter. There must be someone else on this plane great enough to warrant fate.

Or maybe it's a cumulative thing, and this is a whole planeload of ordinary people who've been tempting fate in smallish ways, being brought down together. How efficient.

Nobody good with facts would have spent her career fiddling about with ideas and stories whose reality, unlike Tom's, was only in the mind.

She notices her own past tense. As a teacher, she knows that is a significant alteration in style.

She's so goddamned cold. This can't be happening. There is nothing she can think about, or do, that can make this not be happening.

"Look," says Tom, touching her arm. Yes, there's Sheila, she's made it to the front of their set of rows in this frenzied cabin, and she's standing on something, a seat, waving her arms in broad sweeps like one of those ground crew people guiding a plane to a halt at an airport terminal. In night landings, Lila recalls, there are lights at the ends of those wide, sweeping arms.

And there are terminals. Ground. Warmth and lights. Long waits at customs and at luggage carousels. The slightly odd, stiff feeling of legs moving, feet touching, after so long in the air. The small disorientation of being in one place after so recently being elsewhere.

Barely imaginable. Infinitely desirable.

Not everyone is quick to abandon panic. How ungainly and inelegant people become when they're frightened—where exactly do they think they can scramble to, with everyone sealed up in this soup can? What do they think would happen if they did get out? Are they in such a hurry for that dark, frozen instant? It's a few moments before Sheila, and presumably the other attendants elsewhere, gain some silence and order. Sheila looks, to Lila's eye, scared but holding on. No doubt flight attendants are trained in crisis and control; but the classroom, as Lila well knows herself, isn't preparation for much of anything beyond more classrooms.

If Sheila is scared, must this not be real?

Susie is sobbing, that's one of the remaining sounds. Her mother is stroking her hair and rocking her but looks inattentive, staring blankly ahead. Can Susie tell that her mother isn't quite with her? Does she know there are limits to her protection?

Even so, it would be nice to curl up in protecting arms. Tom's arms would be nice. Ideally, they could cradle each other.

"I'm scared," Susie is wailing. "Make it stop." She speaks, no doubt, for everyone, but Lila wishes she'd be quiet. Some things, it's too much, hearing them said out loud.

"Please," Sheila is calling out, in a carefully non-panicky way. "May I have your attention, please. Could everyone take your seats, please, and listen."

How polite, all those pleases. What a nice child Sheila must have been, so well brought up by, Lila imagines, doting, careful parents. Did they, unlike Tom, want their daughter to be a flight attendant, or would they have pre-ferred law or medicine or motherhood? Were they disap-pointed by her choice, or proud? How sad they will be to have trained their daughter to such responsible polite-ness, and to have it come to this.

So many people don't hear authority in the voices of nice women. Would it help if Lila stood up and shouted, "Everybody, shut fucking up"? Lila had a fairly dainty up-bringing herself, but has overcome it.

Still, Sheila's labours have their effect. Most people, both eager and fearful for word, do settle well enough. Lila's hands tremble and Tom takes one of them, it hardly matters whether to comfort or be comforted himself.

Everyone is looking at Sheila, but the voice, when it comes, is not hers. Nor is it the thin voice of the pilot that they heard after takeoff. What's happened to him, is he just very busy?

No, this voice is deep, soothing and calm. Disembod-ied. Like God beginning to speak all around them.

Well, whoever is up there in the cockpit will have to be pretty god-like, that's for sure. All those hands will need to be terribly adept, their brains unclouded and sharp. They will require a keen sense of reality indeed. Lila is glad she hasn't met or even seen them. It leaves her free to hope and imagine they are much smarter and more powerful and shrewd and rational than anyone she knows.

Anyone who gets them out of this is more than welcome in her living room. They could be her best friends. Anything. She no longer has frivolous criteria, such as affection, for who may enter her house. She just longs to be there herself. Given the chance, she would never leave it again.

"Ladies and gentleman," the voice is saying, slowly and firmly, "may I have your attention." Lila notices he doesn't say please. Most people are quiet, and some, like the big man by the emergency exit, even tip their heads towards the sound. Still, there's whimpering and sobbing here and there, and away on the other side of the cabin and off to the back, somebody is crying out, "No, no, no," over and over. It sounds like an elderly, tremulous, female voice, but might well, in these circumstances, belong to a young, muscular man.

Lila imagines all sorts of appearances boiling away, leaving behind only essences.

"Ladies and gentlemen. This is your co-pilot, Frank McLean, speaking. As you are aware by now, we are experiencing some difficulties." Difficulties! Does he think they are fools? Still, how would Lila put it, in his place? He can hardly say, "Ladies and gentlemen, we've got a nasty little fire going here, and we're about to plummet ten thousand metres, and if the fall doesn't kill you, the landing certainly will."

Oops. "Lila!" Tom is frowning. Did she laugh out loud again?

Sheila has stopped waving her arms and appears to be listening herself. How young she is, at least compared with Lila, if not, say, with Susie. Lila ought to feel grateful to have had so much more time.

Sheila must be pretty brave to stand on that seat, surveying the passengers, probably trying to gauge where trouble may erupt, who is most upset, and in what ways, and how they may have to be dealt with. Trying to look calm and strong herself; although she must also be assessing her own chances, wishing for lost joys, mourning lost years.

Maybe this morning, she was pulling herself slowly from the arms of a suitably young, ardent man, and dressing quietly in the dark, sorry to leave him, trying not to wake him, already missing him.

Or maybe she leapt up happily from her solitary sheets, turning on lights and the radio, dressing quickly, buttoning her blouse and drawing on her stockings, tying that vivid red scarf around her throat with eager fingers, anticipating love in another country at the end of this day.

Or there's Susie, just a little kid, with breasts and pleasures and choices and disasters and passions and pains and regrets all ahead of her. "My ears hurt," she cries from the sanctuary of her mother's arms. "My head hurts. Make it stop." How touching, that sort of faith.

Again, Susie is speaking for everyone, and again, Lila thinks it might be better for some things not to be put right out into the air like that.

It's true there's a drumming, and a kind of heavy sharpness. She sees a few people shaking their heads as if trying to dislodge an irritant, others poking fingers into their ears. Some are yawning, which usually works when pressures are changing. This feeling, whatever it is, isn't actually painful, despite Susie's complaints, but it does seem to create a sort of buzzing. Tom is also frowning and shaking his head. What's on his mind? Their thoughts, his and Lila's, are almost certain to be different in these circumstances.

"Ladies and gentlemen," the deep, dark voice is saying again. It must be nice, Lila thinks, to have so many people hanging on every word. Certainly different from standing in front of a classroom. Of course, this man has a captive audience. Nobody's likely to get bored and wander off.

This time, Tom pokes her. He is really getting annoying. It's her turn to frown. Any relationship is much more than love. It also, if it has any life to it, involves delicate balancings, little tugs and pulls of power, shiftings of position. Briefly, she glares at him, because in love, it's more than love that people need to be alert to.

Still, this is no time to fall out of touch. "Listen," she says, and grips his hand hard.

five

THE VOICE FILLS THE
air of the cabin. Or sucks it out. "What we are dealing
with, as most of you are already aware, involves one of
our engines."

Engines? Lila almost turns to look again: it seemed to
her the trouble was the fire on the wing. But then, engines are probably attached to wings, so any problems
with one will be shared, willy-nilly, with the other. Like
herself and Tom: a disagreement with his wife, or for that
matter a moment of tenderness, naturally slips into Lila's
existence in some unspoken, barely discernible fashion.
Or a truculent student, a difficult paper, an evening or
weekend of missing him, naturally ripples out of her, tipping into him.

And unlike her and Tom (actually more like Tom and
his wife), parts of planes are bolted and welded together.

So of course they affect each other, how stupid of her.

"What some of you have been able to see is a very small amount of fire"—does fire come in amounts?—"and there are several connected issues relating to stability and pressure. Your crew wants to reassure you that these circumstances may appear more serious than they are." May, implying, just as easily, may not. "The important thing at the moment is to remain calm."

Not necessarily. Calm is good, but keeping the plane in the air until it can land safely and peacefully where it's supposed to would be infinitely preferable; which doesn't mean bedlam isn't also dangerous.

"As those of you familiar with this type of aircraft will know," and this does not include Lila, who has no idea what sort of plane they're flying in, except it's big and, she hopes, sturdy, "we have four engines, which means we have flexibility in dealing with that aspect of our current difficulty. So that a problem with one, while unusual and unfortunate, would not be a unique occurrence."

Really? Lila bets it's a unique occurrence to everyone in this cabin, and likely unique to those in the cockpit, as well, unless they've had exceptionally unlucky careers. Some people (her mother was one) find comfort in the notion that at least others are enduring similar, or worse, misfortunes. Lila, on the other hand, considers "I'm not the only one" an odd proposition. It's no help to her if Tom, or Susie and her mother, or the big guy by the emergency exit, go down with her, and her own destination hardly improves theirs. How on earth would it?

"As to the fire itself, we are confident the aircraft's normal design and safety features will deal with that." And what, exactly, does "deal with" mean? This whole speech strikes Lila as ominously padded and fluffy, with too many vague, rolling words and too few crisp-edged, clear ones. She would personally prefer to hear words like "extinguish" or "douse" or simply "put out."

"We also want to assure you that your flight crew is highly experienced and dedicated to the safety of each one of you. Your captain, Luke Thomas, who spoke to you earlier, has been a pilot for eighteen years, and has asked me to advise you that he has every confidence in achieving a safe conclusion to this flight."

Luke Thomas—now there's a solid name, a name to be trusted and reckoned with, a name with hair on its chest, and maybe even its back. Pity about his voice. Lila wonders, do his skills more resemble his name or his voice?

"As well, we are in communication with advisers at our departure location and also with those at several potential destinations, and we are continuing to evaluate a number of alternatives. You will be told of any decisions that affect you, for instance if a different landing location, such as Reykjavik in Iceland, is determined to be preferable to Heathrow." Small subsidiary sounds of discontent rise up among his listeners; the thought of Iceland as distressing as the ocean? Surely not.

"Meanwhile, rest assured everything possible is being done." Lila hears mournful medical tones trying to cushion bad news: "We're doing everything possible," a sentence, in her small experience, of virtually certain doom.

That small experience came during three brief, endless days between the morning her brother's child was hit by a car and the late afternoon he died—doctors and nurses repeating and repeating those words, necessary but unbearable to hear.

Unbearable, also, watching over the tiny blond three-year-old who had been lively and glinting but now was abruptly broken and wired, tubed and wrecked. Lila, leaning over him, recalled with regret her irritation at his loud, high voice and his recklessness with delicate objects. His gravest recklessness, it now turned out, was with himself.

Poor helpless Sam, gazing up, wondering why the people he trusted didn't just fix him; as Susie, wrapped whimpering in her mother's arms, may be wondering much the same thing.

No one could fix anything. Don and his wife, Alice, couldn't fix themselves or each other, both blaming Alice, although more or less silently, for their darting child's impulse to dodge between parked cars into the street. The horrified, trembling driver of the car that hit him said, and the police agreed, that there was nothing that could have been done.

The only thing that could have been done was to keep him safer, hold him closer, not let the eye wander for even an instant, and this his mother had failed to do. Naturally his mother. Lila thought it could as easily have been his father, Don, her brother, except he was at work and free of keeping an eye, keeping near.

Lila loves her brother, although she doesn't always entirely like him, and imagines he feels similarly about her. She liked Alice well enough, a nice woman of modest, ruined hopes. She had struck Lila before this event as wispy and undefined, but her suffering turned out to be not wispy at all. It was loud and terrible and could not be helped, her grief rolling far beyond words into raw, howling purity. Don just rocked, arms clutching only himself.

If Lila could hardly contain herself and her helplessness to repair or undo, it must have been immeasurably worse for Alice and Don. Each of them. They remained separate in the aftermath, too, Alice with her splayed anguish, Don with his pale, silent mourning and evident blame.

In the long hospital hours, Alice and Don waited, waited, refusing to change clothes, or to eat, or to rest;

whereas to Lila it seemed urgent to go home and then reappear showered and clean, in sharply ironed outfits, as if order of even that ordinary sort could restore order in the rest of their disrupted universe.

Everything was vivid beyond endurance; nothing could be muted, dimmed, turned down. The moment Lila stepped off the elevator at Sam's hospital floor, piercing smells cut at her nostrils, and high, remote lights began assaulting her eyes. The crispness of starched uniforms on nurses hurrying through corridors came to her ears as rasping, maddening static.

The words she mainly remembers are: "We're doing everything we can" and "Everything possible is being done."

"These awful things happen," people said. "Tragic, just a terrible, tragic accident." All true words. Obviously there are limits to what true words can repair.

Like Don, Lila was furious with grief; but while his rage was mainly at Alice, Lila's was at unfairness, the betrayal of assumptions and hopes, and at sorrow itself: Don's, Alice's and, most profoundly, Sam's.

Lila hasn't seen Alice since the divorce twelve years ago. She often sees Don and his second wife, Anne, and their three children, two daughters and a little boy. They are lovely kids, friendly as puppies. Lila is a more patient and attentive aunt than she used to be, as Don is a more patient and attentive father.

Robbie's four now, so has already outlived Sam. There's no forgetting, but life does go on, reconfiguring itself, patching over even the worst leaks and gaps that occur.

As it would go on without Lila, no question.

Who would miss her?

Tom, she hopes, would top the mourning list, if he weren't right here beside her. Otherwise, mainly, Patsy and Nell, sturdy comrades of years of laughter, achievements, sorrows, misunderstandings, secrets, and gallons of chocolate, oceans of wine.

Tears come to her own eyes, preparing to miss them.

But that's stupid. If she dies, she'll be gone and won't miss a thing. She hopes they'd miss her, though. And she'd have gone in such a spectacular way, there'd be that to remember as well. She would be an actual story, a character in a lively, public event, not merely a fond, personal memory.

Poor Tom, he must be considering entirely different family matters.

"At the same time," the voice is continuing, "since we should be prepared for all eventualities, our flight attendants will shortly be repeating and augmenting their earlier safety instructions and pointing out emergency precautions and equipment. They would be grateful for your complete attention." No problem this time, Lila bets. Everyone will be riveted, and no one will consider the attendants' gestures outlandish.

"Again, let me assure you we have full confidence in landing safely, and ask that everyone continue to act in a calm and responsible fashion. There is nothing to be gained by becoming overly concerned about difficulties that will almost certainly be resolved."

He sounds to Lila like a man hedging his bets, that "almost" a dead giveaway.

So to speak. But she mustn't laugh.

Tom's hand is no longer exactly holding hers, it's just kind of lying there, limp. Sometimes, on those rare occasions they've been able to sleep together overnight, she has wakened with a feeling of being smothered, controlled by an arm or a leg slung heavily across her, and has needed frantically, carefully, to ease herself free.

Perhaps instead, she should have cultivated the ability to endure being pinned.

"Please stay in your seats and ensure your seatbelts are fastened. After their safety demonstration, your flight attendants will be offering soft drinks, coffee and tea, compliments of the airline. They will not be serving further alcoholic beverages, as we're sure you will understand. The attendants will also endeavour to answer any questions you may have, but they may not be fully able to do so. The aircraft is complex and so, of course, are some of the measures being taken to ensure our safe arrival."

Good to know there are measures, however complex. Lila would surely be stumped if she had to figure out how to put out a blaze on the wing of an airplane, not to mention deal with whatever problems the fire is a symptom of, but if there are ways to do so, it's excellent somebody knows them.

Perhaps there's a manual. Maybe in the cockpit, crew members are thumbing through frantically in search of the page that gives them the particular answer to this particular disaster.

"Eject," it might say. "Give up and get out."

The big man by the emergency exit is sitting up taller, filling the space even more than before and turning this way and that to survey what's around him. He looks like a man who intends to look after himself. Lila has seen that kind of expression before on the faces of men: closed in, removed, hard.

Lila is not bad herself at being imposing when that's called for; it's not solely a matter of size. There's no way of knowing how useful that's likely to be, but at least it's a skill. In fact she has plenty of talents; only, some of her most prized ones aren't necessarily the ones that will come in most handy today.

She would say she is adaptable, fairly affectionate and a swift, cool analyst of some matters. She is pretty good at both hope and forgetfulness, which so often rely on each other. She is no use whatever at concrete skills like wiring or carpentry. She has read largely and widely, but can't, off the top of her head, recall any literature that would very usefully apply to the moment.

If it's not too much trouble, she tries to be nice. She also has an aptitude for ruthlessness when it has seemed to her to be required. And on and on. There is simply no way to tell what characteristics are useful today, and which may do harm to the cause of survival.

"Anyone with special concerns, such as a medical problem, should alert a flight attendant. Your crew will update you on our progress as developments occur. Thank you for your attention." Abruptly there's a click, and the deep, assured voice is gone. Lila feels a tick in her heart of something like grief for its loss. Others may feel this, as well. People turn to each other, and there are renewed sounds of panic.

This is the kind of event that must elicit extremes. Whatever is at the very core and root of each human here will be called out, and called upon. Someone with a cheerier view of the nature of humans might feel safe, even protected, facing crisis in the company of so many. To Lila, it feels dangerous.

It's true not all the seats were filled for this flight, so there are slightly fewer concerns than there might have been. At least there's no one beside her in the window seat climbing or screeching or clawing to get out. Or, for that matter, patting her hand, speaking softly. But there are nevertheless many, many people, each an unknown quantity, in a space which was adequate for its original purpose but is entirely inadequate for explosions of despair and terror, or even great bursts of generosity and goodness.

As long as they were sitting neatly in rows, facing forward, eating and drinking, talking or reading or napping, merely passing dull hours, they were just people headed in a common direction, with their own stories and for individual reasons. Now, though, it could actually make a difference if Susie's mother's devotion to her child were so radical it caused her to abduct her. It might certainly make a difference if the man by the emergency exit really is the sort of fellow who could have murdered his wife last night.

What if civility does vanish in bits and pieces, as on Lila's television screen, until it ends up in some blood-drenched horror? What if she was right, that just under civility's thin skin there's destruction wanting out, waiting for an excuse to unleash itself, inflict revenge?

Revenge for what? For grievances, deprivations and indignities, or, in this instance, terror—all those things that boil up beneath that fragile and transparent surface.

Not yet, though. So far there is upheaval, but not real destruction. Close by, someone is moaning, or praying, "Oh God, oh God." Some people's lips move silently, some are fingering beads of one kind and another, and who knows what others are doing beneath beards or veils?

If they go down, it will be, Lila thinks, quite a representative, multicultural crash, demographically speaking.

There may, for all she knows, be cultural as well as individual differences in how people react to a threat to their lives. An added potential discordance. At any rate, there are dangers inside and out.

Miraculous, really, how small the world has become, so that people from practically anywhere can, with more luck than they're having today, be practically anywhere else in just a few hours, and can speak to each other in a matter of seconds. People from practically anywhere can find themselves facing death together in a single compact, narrow space.

"What a world," Lila says.

"What?"

This would be fascinating if one were, say, God: able to peer into these people and this singular event to see what evolves. A kind of scientific experiment controlled in one petri-dish place.

"What do you think?" she asks Tom, who is surely experienced in the careful scrutiny of nuance and sorting fact from hope—what else must politicians gauge all the time? Although as a politician he did miscalculate; in the end, he did lose.

Think, if voters had decided differently that day, Tom wouldn't be sitting here beside her now. And there'd be no reason for her to be here either, in his absence. Imagine that. One election six years ago, and here they are now.

Many other factors are also involved, of course; it can't be entirely the fault of Tom's former constituents.

"What do I think about what?"

Can that be irritation in his tone? How—tiny of him.

Heavens, he looks awful. Bloodshot and shaky, as if he hasn't slept for days. From pain, from knifing cramps, Lila has fainted three times in her life, and imagines that just beforehand she must have looked much the way he does now. Fainting feels exactly like what it is: nourishing blood rushing away from the brain, leaving airiness, absence; and down you go.

Here there's no room to fall, except slightly forward or gently sideways.

"Tom? What's the matter?"

Funny how even in extraordinary situations, common, daily sorts of questions pop out. As if he'd just shown up at her door looking wan after a tough day of classes.

Most weeknights they're both free; they recover from their days in Lila's cool and quiet living room, its pale greys-blues-greens broken by fat flashy cushions, strokes of red and yellow vividness, rather like Sheila's flamboyant scarf with her military-style uniform.

It's a small house, Lila's, but it's her own, and dear lord she'd like to be in it right now. It's a little messy upstairs in her office, scattered with papers and essays and lists of marks, but otherwise it is mainly serene, and safe, within reason.

Tom, on the other hand, does go on sometimes about his mortgage, and repairs, and alterations. Naturally his place is bigger than hers; it has had to contain more.

"It's gauche, I expect," he has told her, "but I've always picked up some small thing from every trip I've been on, and I have a whole room of stuff now, with just a couple of chairs. All the walls and shelves have sketches and carvings and bits and pieces to remind me of a particular event. So I can go into that room and see my whole life. The travelling parts, anyway."

Many tales in one crowded room, evidently.

And what would he take back for that room from this trip? What, someday, might he see on a shelf to remind him of Lila?

"Hardly gauche," she said. "It sounds rather nice. I have things from my travels, as well, but nothing so determined." She has tended to count on memory—of Paul's lean limbs, of the spot Virginia walked into the water weighted with stones, of egg sandwiches on a French train, of chanted echoes in vaulting cathedrals, of smells and colours, crowds and companions and moments of solitude—rather than memorabilia; but who knows if that was wise?

If they survive this, it will not have been a trip requiring a souvenir to keep it vivid.

"I see myself as an old man sitting in one of those chairs, looking around and remembering everything and being grateful for so much." Lila wondered if he pictured his wife in the other chair. She wondered if his wife also collected memories of journeys, in the form of, say, carvings, or tapestries. Perhaps that's what got her interested in crafts in the first place.

In Tom and Lila's earlier days, they closed her front door behind them and steamed to her bedroom, tossing off covers and clothes. More recently, having become sedate (or regrettably accustomed), they've been as likely to sit on her pearly-grey sofa discussing their days over drinks, exchanging work worries, offering suggestions and tactics. On good days Lila has set out cheese and biscuits, but after ones spent watching ideas and words ricochet off particularly impenetrable students, she might just dump chips into a bowl. Tom mixes drinks.

Once, she called this time "a sort of picture frame around each day," and he nodded. Still, it was different from clutching at each other in cars and barely making it home. There were some startled moments in those days, catching sight of steamed windows. Surprised by herself, she'd said, "This is very bad."

"Positively adolescent." He grinned.

"If we get caught, people will think we're ridiculously old to be necking in cars."

"If we get caught, they'll be extremely impressed."

She was rather impressed herself. And skittish, as he must have been, too, because really, jokes aside, getting caught would be awful. Some people would be thrilled, a few gravely injured. Mainly, events would unfold and occur that would be out of their hands.

There are serious consequences to desire, although it isn't easy always to keep them in mind.

There must be rumours. In the close, peculiar setting of the campus, neither affection nor hostility goes unnoticed. Tom and Lila have counted on the many possibilities for misinterpretation, and the unlikelihood of proof. Except for when they've been overcome, they've been tremendously clever.

Now this, though.

They have continued to be overcome sometimes, but mainly in private. They might spend hours on her sofa discussing their respective days, their work, their students, their frustrations and their different fields of interest, and drinking, watching television, commenting on this and that (like massacres, like blood), but they also continue to slide into her dark, muffled bedroom, to tear, carefully, at each other's clothes, and to fall around each other with happy lust. They have been attentive to each other's desires, in Lila's view. Not all her lovers have been as clever as Tom.

Eventually he has roused himself to drive into the night, home to what remains of his family. To the no-longer-depressed Dorothy, that handy, surprisingly capable businesswoman. In high school, where Tom and Dorothy met, she was apparently a cheerleader named Dot, but it wouldn't be fair, years later, to hold that against her. Only it's been hard not to take silent jabs; just to let some of the air out.

"The thing is, Lila," Tom explained (or tried to explain, she wasn't a very sympathetic listener), "she and I have known each other so long and been through so much. A lot of feelings may be different now, but I can't throw out a whole history." A kind of amputation, Lila supposed, not a surgery happily undertaken even for the sake of substantial rewards.

Naturally, the words "have cake, eat it too" sprang to mind, but then, many words came to mind.

Anyway, it's necessary to give attention to what is, not always what is not; if for no other reason than to avoid becoming one of those people who moan and grieve about flawed parents, faulty childhoods, rotten teachers, crazy bosses, blaming and blaming, no mercy at all.

Unless actual crimes are involved, Lila has little patience with that. Her own parents were flawed, and her own childhood faulty, and exactly whose isn't? But look at what became of her; at what, good and bad, they helped her become.

As Tom quite properly and frequently says—although not, as it happens, in these circumstances today—"We should enjoy what we do have, not regret what we don't."

For the most part, it seems to Lila, he is, stubbornly and unreasonably, an optimist. Unlike her, he doesn't often, on the road to cheer, get tripped up, waylaid, by a dissenting and unruly mind.

They may have different outlooks, but nevertheless they do have much in common: their talents, for one thing, which lean more towards consuming than creating. Lila has laboured over two books of textual scrutiny and no broad fascination—who in the larger world especially cares about comparative influences of rural and urban geographies in particular novels by English and North American women?—although they were interesting enough to her, and excellent exercises. Tom tosses off (although he does not, he crafts them slowly and scrupulously, sometimes phoning her in search of just the right verb) his political analyses for various media, but she doesn't think either of them could say they've actually *made* much of anything, not from scratch, starting from nothing.

Also, they both live by their wits. Their hands are smooth, their bodies relatively unmuscled, but Lila imagines their brains toughened and calloused and wiry with regular and strenuous use.

At the moment she'd like to be able to shut off her mind, let it go limp, but it doesn't seem to work that way.

Tom's mind is another matter. Here's something she's never seen before: his eyes open so wide the white shows all the way around the irises. He looks like descriptions she's read of terrified horses trapped in a barn fire. Horses apparently panic and don't know how to escape. They lose their heads in smoke.

Perhaps she should slap him. She owes him one.

What will she do if he turns out to be one of the people here who fall apart, come unstuck, implode, explode, whatever?

On the other hand, she hasn't begun to imagine how to be, herself. Some previously unknown, unfamiliar aspect may well, for all she knows, tap-tap its way to the top.

Leaning towards him, she puts a hand on each of his. At least they're together. They've had their ups and downs, and it's each other's fault they're here in the first place, but if there's any comfort at all, it's that he's beside her.

Sort of beside her. Beside her in his fashion. "Sorry," he says finally. A faint flush of blood is returning, and he's losing that ridiculous pop-eyed look. He looks towards her; not quite at her, though. As if he is embarrassed by something that just occurred in his own private life, his eyes are cast down and shifting.

Well. She certainly knows that expression, and this is really, seriously, not a good time for it. Her own eyes narrow, she removes her hands, but perhaps, since he isn't looking directly at her, he doesn't catch the warning.

Or doesn't care. Other interests may be overriding. For instance: "I have something to tell you," he said cautiously one evening as they sat on her sofa doing that picture-frame thing around their day. "I'm going to be away all next week." He was looking down at, possibly, her knees.

This was a Thursday. "When? What for?"

"On the weekend, I guess. A little tour to visit the girls, a quick family whip-round."

"You guess? What does that mean? When did you decide?" His little surprises have often been blows to her heart, leaving her bruised and breathless in the first moments after impact.

"I didn't, actually. Decide, I mean. Only, Dorothy misses the girls, and she thinks Angela has some trouble she won't talk about on the phone, so she decided we ought to go see her, and while we were at it we could fit Peggy in, too, with a bit of extra driving."

Angela is the daughter who made Tom a grandfather; another family time, bitter for Lila (and it would be banal, if accurate, to note that shortly afterwards she was flying to her own conference in England and the surprising, temporary embraces of the academic Paul).

Peggy is at university, studying something incomprehensible to do with mathematics, although, as Tom says, "I have no idea where she would have gotten such a mind. It's very pure and abstract, her sort of math. I don't even know if it's proper to call it math, or if it's something far more rarefied than that. At any rate it involves a great many numbers and odd symbols, and I haven't a clue. She speaks of doing something with computers. It's very strange, Lila, to feel your children going places you can't imagine. You take them so far, and then you just stare at their backs while they tear off into a whole different universe."

Certainly Angela has the more comprehensible life. Or, as Tom put it, "She's a lot like her mother."

Bite your tongue, Lila.

"And this trip was decided on when?"

He waved one hand vaguely. "Oh, just recently. The last few days, I guess. Dorothy organized it. She talked to them." Sometimes he has made himself sound so help-less, so much a pawn in the hands of powerful women, including herself, that Lila could kick him.

She could also have wept, but mainly, and she thought men didn't often understand this, out of rage. Maybe women didn't understand all that often, either, that when they cried, it was more as an alternative to hurling glasses or fists than as an expression of grief. And that grief and anger often dance together in the heart.

So he would spend a week in the company of his wife, visiting the two young women they had created and raised. They would hear the same words, see the same views, and would speak later in the car, in bed, of what they'd heard and seen. Tom feigned surprise that any of this should upset Lila. His crafted gestures of amazement were, she thought, extremely chilly and very clever.

At such times the two of them have presented most unattractive faces to each other. They have been saved, she expects, by a mutual disbelief that these are each other's true faces, except at small and particular mo-ments.

They do not quarrel well. They would be poor exam-ples for books on how to argue.

What a thing, that there actually are books on how to quarrel, not to mention manuals for almost every other kind of human action. And people write and read these things.

They're missing a market, though, for more important challenges. She can't think of a single guide to how to starve, or flee a war, or go down gracefully in a burning plane. The sort of book that could come in truly handy.

Actually, she had a pretty good time the week he was gone, out playing at movies and bars with Patsy and Nell. She was slightly worried he might also be experiencing unexpected pleasures in this absence from each other.

She wouldn't mistake temporary lightness for a permanent desire, but was afraid he might.

He phoned when he got back to town. "Jesus, Lila, I missed you." And there they were again, until the next time he couldn't quite look her in the eye. Like now.

"Sorry," he repeats. "What were you saying?"

"I was asking what you thought."

"About what?"

Good lord. "About what's happening. What's likely to happen. About what the co-pilot was talking about, and whether we'll make it or not. All this," and she waves her arm vaguely, intending to encompass her concerns about the likely nature of a mass of varied humans in a small and dangerous space.

"Oh god." He shakes his head. "I don't know." Now what the hell is this about—he's finally looking at her, but appears to have flown into a fury. With her? "But I wish to god I wasn't here."

"Yes. Well. I expect you have plenty of company there."

Her voice was too dry, she supposes. Less than soothing.

"What the hell do you keep finding so funny?" His voice is cutting and she flinches. Then she is furious, too—how dare he cause her to flinch? What does he want from her? If she can't make little jokes, what's she supposed to do with all her bubbling disbelief and terror? If these things are going to bubble, they might as well roll out as laughter. Considering the alternatives.

Still. This isn't like the two of them getting so huffy he can march out her door for a comfortable return to his own, other life, while she slams doors in her house. This isn't a case of having a chance to reunite later. "We ought to be able to comfort each other better," she has suggested more than once. If they had taken her advice to heart, they'd have had more practice by now.

"Actually," she says quietly, "I don't find it funny at all." She touches fingers to his knee, hoping the gesture can't be mistaken for the sort of placating move she associates with women fearing injury. "I'm only trying to work out what's going on and how to be prepared and how not to be crazy. At least we're together. Whatever happens, we can maybe try to help each other. That's something, isn't it?"

She is proud of herself for this, feels extremely mature. Camouflaging huge emotions, feigning others, seems often enough the very definition of maturity.

"Christ." He shakes his head. "What's going to happen?"

He can't imagine she would know; but she keeps her fingers on his knee, and her voice light. "That's what I was trying to work out, from what he said. Some kind of formula to decode, a sort of arithmetic, I thought. Subtract the need to keep people calm from what's actually wrong, add a bit of hope and multiply the skill involved— if we could figure out the formula, we might be able to tell what the odds are." She shrugs. "I don't know."

"Disaster." He is muttering more to himself than to her. "It's a fucking disaster."

Oh. Now she sees what he's talking about. Not death so much as the debris.

Yes, they've mainly been careful, and lucky as well. But now here they are, indisputably together. Is there an explanation some kind friend or ally might come up with to account for this? Tom has the flimsy excuse of a conference, but Lila has no possible purpose for being here. And if she had, what are the odds they'd be beside each other on the same plane? And have booked the same return flight as well?

Still, people believe what they want to. What they need to.

She can certainly see that, for Tom, this may be a fuck-ing disaster, all right, in a number of ways.

If they go down spectacularly together today, they might just as well have stripped off in a campus courtyard between classes, and embraced, and caressed, and licked each other's nipples, and laid each other gently on the sunny bricks.

Right at the moment, she can't quite make out his features, but surely that's only tears, not an absence of love. Which is funny, since she is not a weeper, at any rate in public. "I can't save us," she says, without quite knowing what she means. "But we could help." Each other, but she already said that.

"No." He sounds exhausted. "You're right. We should never have started."

Did she say anything remotely to that effect? She can't recall it, but perhaps she did; or something similar, and sufficiently vague that he could misinterpret.

And what does he mean, should never have started? Started what, the conversation? The trip? Their entire time together, the whole five-decimal-five years they've had their scraped-together, by-and-large precious, mirac-ulous, middle-aged, greying, pot-bellied, skin-crumpled, joyous moments?

How easily, lightly, selfishly he tosses regret and grief in her direction.

That's certainly something new to know about him. Ordinarily, she assumes any knowledge will find a useful place for itself sometime, somewhere, but what exactly is she supposed to do with understanding that he doesn't want to die with her? That right to the last, hurtling through sunlight and over streaks of clouds, sitting beside a flaming wing in this potential wreckage, it's the secret that's important.

And that whether they wind up shattered or brilliantly,

gratefully whole, they are surely exposed, and he is ruined, and he cares that he's ruined.

Already in the other world miles away and down, their situation is drawing attention. It's known about at, apparently, several airports and by various experts in the field of flights and airplanes. Almost certainly, information is being picked up on emergency bands and monitors. Perhaps at this moment phone calls are going out to their nearest and dearest, or at least to their closest relatives and flight insurance beneficiaries.

Word will be simply in the air, spreading in its normal quick and mysterious ways; not unlike flames.

Does he really imagine she would spend what may be her own last moments fretting over his exposure in the hearts of other people? What must he think of her? Who does he suppose she is?

Perhaps he believes she is good. Good, in the sense of being a whole-hearted altruist. In terms of having no being whatever, none of her own interests or concerns. All this time, has he mistaken her for a mutant Mother Teresa?

"Jesus. I cannot imagine what you keep finding to laugh about."

Well, for one thing, that they're going to go down, if they do, with the same ridiculous, irreconcilable dilemma they've always had: the struggle between his interests and hers.

Lila would hate it if Tom crashed in a plane with his wife. She would drive herself crazy with pictures of their last, desperately intimate moments.

It would certainly be ironic if Dorothy drives herself crazy with pictures of Tom and Lila's last desperately intimate moments. Because right now Lila is as angry with him as she has ever been. Jammed together, she thinks they could scarcely be more remote from each other. She could hurt him, very badly. She could just weep.

ON THIS MILD, BRIGHT
June day, Lila could have been poking around in her garden, mowing her small lawn, leaning her face up into
sunshine. Enjoying an ease, if not exactly a joy, she might
barely have noticed.

Now she can no longer quite believe in a life beyond
this narrow, catastrophic space. A few hours ago, when
the plane lifted off, houses grew tiny, roads shrank, land-
scape diminished, finally disappearing under the first
wispy cloud layers. In just that way, other possibilities
have now also receded, grown tiny.

And she is in this enormous rage.

If they survive, if that co-pilot is right and the odds
aren't entirely bad, what does she do then?

She could break Tom's bones for insufficient love. She
could break her own for enjoying ease, if not exactly joy,
and barely noticing.

They have been glaring at each other, hard. Now, finally, his eyes drop. "I'm sorry," he says. "I don't know what came over me." He looks older than he did a few hours ago, a different man from the one standing eagerly, nervously, at her front door this morning.

This morning!

The edges of his eyes, the sides of his mouth, have started to fall. At this rate he'll look like a basset before this is done. Does she look like an aging stranger to him?

"Lila? I'm sorry. Really."

Apology or regret? There's quite a difference.

"It's fine" she says, although it's not. He looks happier. Good for him.

He's been her lover, not her enemy. But at this moment their history doesn't apply, and something is certainly hostile.

This space? Her body has been folded for ages into its narrow seat, beyond which is Tom, and then the narrow aisle, and then more rows of people in, or scrambling around and out of, their own narrow seats. There's no room to move, and no place to escape to. Tom has his briefcase tucked under the seat, as Lila has her shoulder bag tucked beneath the one ahead of her. Other people have cluttered their small spaces with sweaters, toys, books, bags and computers, all the detritus of a disrupted journey; and overhead in storage, who knows? There could be anything up there.

Crazy people used to be wrapped into straitjackets—does that still happen? They were as bound and swaddled as babies, as trussed as turkeys, so radically immobilized they must have wanted to burst out of their skins.

"Lila?" Tom is saying. "You okay? Truly, I'm sorry."

"Sure," she says vaguely. "I know."

When she was alive, Lila's mother was an irritatingly

dab hand with the banal. "Idle hands are the devil's workshop," she liked to say, bustling around her kitchen, her yard, her town, intent on tidy good works of one sort or another. And on the same theme, "If you keep busy, there's no time to brood." Lila's mother apparently found her broody, which made Lila feel rather hen-like, in a lethargic, sedentary sort of way.

Or as if she contained some hard, fragile, out-of-proportion *thing*, which at some point would require painful release.

Once again Lila thinks, *I want*, but still cannot find an object for the verb.

What would her mother have had to say about this situation, in which there's little choice about having idle hands, except in the cockpit, where Lila hopes hands are being quite busy and useful?

Her mother scrubbed floors on her knees and vacuumed ferociously. Or she set off briskly, in her click-clicking heels, clip-on earrings swinging time, to spend a morning or afternoon visiting one or another sad or sick person. Even then, Lila recognized the anger, although unable to identify its source.

"Poor soul," her mother would remark, shaking her head. "We're very lucky, compared with that poor soul." Who might be temporarily or terminally ill, or recently bereaved or abandoned, or just permanently embittered and cranky.

All this fuelled Lila's mother in what Lila considered a slightly creepy way: as if, while doing good, her mother was taking nourishment, as well, like a vampire or a vulture, from the disasters of others. Also, when Lila was very little and had to go along, she disliked the smells of some of those houses. Not dirty, necessarily, or connected with, say, decaying leftovers; rather, smells she came to associate with defeated humans.

"That's a very nasty thing to mention," her mother told her. She meant the smells, not defeat.

Between a mother and a daughter (Lila cannot speak for sons) lies a whole literature of longing and judgment. Mothers and daughters scrutinize each other, hoping for the best, and sharpening knives and lives on the worst. Fathers, especially quiet, kind, inscrutable ones who watch a lot of television, and spend much time in the basement repairing household items, and then die in their fifties, don't stand a chance.

"My mother says your mother's a saint," a child in public school told Lila. "I think she's nice, too." So she was. "You're lucky." So Lila was.

Lila first learned the language of ambivalence and ambiguity not, after all, from stories, but at her mother's knee. A girl who has questions about her mother's obvious virtues is unlikely to become an incurious, naive or patient woman.

Curiosity, scepticism and impatience are not inconsiderable gifts, and Lila is grateful.

Her mother, Lila heard when she was grown and gone, was proud enough of her, although continued to consider her broody and not very useful. And true enough, in a really difficult life, Lila would not have done well. She would have been hard pressed, for instance, to make a living serving in a restaurant, or at the check-out of a supermarket, and certainly she would have been a ridiculously inept refugee. She lacks her mother's experience, it turns out, in performing hard and necessary acts, and has been, as her mother suspected, too indulged when it comes to the point; as it may now be doing.

And so here she sits, furious as a child.

She smiles, very carefully, at Tom, who looks heartbreakingly relieved.

Either her own childishness or her rage may have brought her mother to mind. But also perhaps all those busy good works, the houses and rooms they entered together, the smells of various sufferings—it's here, too, the contained stench of human desires and terrors and sorrows.

The house Lila grew up in had another smell, slightly sulphurous.

"Keeping busy," her mother used to say, "keeps your mind off things." Whatever those things were that couldn't bear the weight of her attention, so that it had to keep flitting, propelling her into those uncountable hours of visiting the variously pathetic and undertaking vast amounts of minimalist, intricate dusting.

She danced so carefully, to avoid landing on the terrible, soft, crushable places of her existence.

Something to do with love, Lila supposes: not enough, not the right kind. Only a failure of love, in Lila's experience, has such frantic effects.

Her mother even rocked Lila hard, that's one of her first memories: being held close, which was nice, but with her head whirling from the speed of the rocking chair whipping forward and back, her mother's faltering soprano lickety-splitting through a lullaby.

"Seething" is the word that comes to Lila's mind; a burning under the surface, not conducive to anyone's comfort or rest.

This may not be true, it may only be Lila's impression. But if it is true, what pain the woman, who after all was far more than only Lila's mother, must have lived with, and how grateful she may have been for the heart attack that deadened all that sizzling.

Lila, considerably seething and sizzling herself, finally finds herself, at this very late date, in complete accord with her mother. She, too, feels the need to act, to move, perhaps vacuum the aisles, dust the seats, scrub the over-head lockers.

Lucky Sheila, standing up there waving her arms, pointing out once again the emergency exits, and where oxygen masks will fall from, and how to retrieve the life-saving cushions, and those lines in the aisles that will still be bright guides in the event of darkness.

"Excuse me." Lila releases her seatbelt, starts to stand.

"What? Where are you going?"

To dust, to vacuum, to scrub, to move faster than her thoughts can follow. "To the washroom."

Tom leans into the aisle, craning to look back. "There's a line-up, and a lot of shit going on. Some wired-up people. You might want to wait. Or shall I come with you?"

A kind enough offer; he has no idea, does he?

"No, the line-up's probably permanent. I might as well join it." She edges, coolly courteous, past his knees.

What she wants urgently to do is to pace, to stretch, to walk and walk, feet pounding on pavement, the firm feel of ground.

Oh, the firm feel of ground! Imagine that.

There's no way to do any sort of brisk circuit. It's more than a line of people waiting for the washroom, there are people crowded in small arm-waving, wild-eyed, frantic-voiced groups in the aisles, leaning over, reaching out—just, Lila supposes, trying as she is to let off steam in a space where there's no outlet for steam.

One man has grabbed another by the neck of his shirt, and is shaking him, shouting. What for?

Well, rage. Much like Lila's own.

What are those men to each other, that they care enough to come to blows? Not lovers, she thinks; perhaps rivals of one kind or another.

Whatever desires and burdens came on board with

each of these people will be heightened and tightened to a thin, high screech.

The thing is, once it's released, how is fury recaptured? Or panic, or any strong feeling; love, too, is hard to restrain. On the best of days it's a challenge to steer sprawling desires into acceptable channels.

Although there is a point to the effort—look at those men wrestling each other, that's just ridiculous, surely. Probably.

Lila is suddenly terribly sad for the ways she has squeezed capacities and desires into a shape far smaller than she once had in mind. She never meant to be reconciled. She never intended to dodge disappointment by not hoping too much.

Poor petrified passengers. Poor Lila, poor Tom, poor survivors left behind on the ground. What a leisurely disaster this is, real, exquisite cruelty. She could almost admire the creative effort involved in devising such a delicate torment.

Someone who hasn't made it to the washroom has thrown up in the aisle, so that people have to step over and around the mess. Another chore for Sheila and her colleagues; or Lila could offer to clean it up herself, keeping very, very busy.

There are six people ahead of her in what appears to be the washroom line—wouldn't it be just her luck for the plane to go down the moment she's finally peeing.

She keeps staring at the skin on her hands. It doesn't look at all the way she imagined it would when she died. She imagined it deeply lined, and thin as an onion layer. That's because she expected to die years and years from now, not necessarily happily, or pleasantly, but at least vaguely far off in the future. She also imagined that by that time there'd be some learned grace, some sense made: a tidy gift, with a tidy bow, by the end. That's how dim and tender the picture was.

Instead here she is, in terrible danger of ending unprepared in the middle, no grace or tidiness or tenderness involved.

An orange-red-coloured vision keeps flaring up, then vanishing; as if there's a rolling metal shutter in her brain, the kind shop-owners pull down over their storefronts in bad neighbourhoods at the end of the day. Only intruders with welding torches get through.

The flaming wing of the plane is a welding torch. It doesn't bear looking at.

To this point in her life, terror has been mainly a vicarious matter: a cheap thrill at a bad movie, a horrid thrill in a great book. Those are, as it turns out, nothing at all like the blank, desperate shock of the real thing.

Partly the fault, perhaps, of her too-ardent, old-fashioned attachment to words. Someone younger, like Sheila, more accustomed to visuals, may be seeing quite well: as if this is a movie she has already watched, whose awful pictorial outcome is already showing in some internal screening room. Or it's a hellish rock video.

The woman ahead of her is also younger than Lila. She looks maybe thirty, and has long hair of a colour people used to call "dirty-blond," although Lila doesn't know why, it's not dirty at all. Her hand, reaching up to brush the hair away from her face, trembles badly, and her wide eyes catch Lila's.

"Hi," she says, voice trembling too. She reaches out her hand in what, here, seems a parody of politeness. "I'm Sarah."

"And I'm Lila. This is something, isn't it?" Talk about parodies!—but it isn't easy finding the right thing to say. Etiquette must be devised on the fly, as it were.

The woman looks almost as startled as Tom did by

Lila's giggle, although thankfully not as irritated. "Sorry," Lila says. "I'm a bit nervous."

"Yeah, I'm freaked. I can't fucking believe this." The voice is harsh and light, an odd combination—it can't be its normal tone.

"I can't, either." This is true, but how—tepid Lila sounds, as if she is a repressed, unpassionate professor of, oh, English literature, what else? Not of anything useful, no clever field that could either explain this or rescue them.

Sarah has, Lila thinks, the narrow, stretched look that predicts a certain ropiness about the neck and arms and thighs by the time she gets to Lila's age. An age she is now not entirely likely to reach. She has a glorious array of freckles on her face and arms, probably elsewhere as well. A few of the freckles duck back into dimples when she abruptly breaks into a grin.

"Weird, huh? Introducing ourselves like we're at a party? Shaking hands over a puddle of barf? You in a hurry for the can?"

"Not really. I mostly just wanted to stand up and stretch."

"Me too. I couldn't sit still. Now I can't stand still. I keep wanting to break out. Like"—she grins again—"*that's* a good idea. I've always got a ton of energy, and usually that's great because I get a lot done and I don't get tired, but this is driving me nuts."

Indeed, she is bouncing on her feet, almost hopping in the aisle. She is very appealing, although Lila can see she is also likely exhausting. Lila spots her wedding ring and wonders if, in her absence, Sarah's husband is enjoying a restful silence. She feels, beside Sarah, unfrenzied, unoccupied. "What do you do?"

"Receptionist for a doctor. Boy, that gets crazy. I was really looking forward to being away. My little sister's in

England, she's going to university there and I haven't seen her for ages." Her expression crumples. "Oh gosh." Lila touches her arm. "My husband said I should come, he's an electrician so he said for a couple of weeks he'd cut back so he could look after the kids after school, stuff like that." Sarah goes so pale her freckles look ready to leap off her skin. "What's he going to do?" she cries. "If I don't come back, what'll they do?" She clutches at Lila. "Do you think people know? I mean our families, will they be told what's going on?"

"I don't know. I was wondering that myself. Maybe not. What could anyone say? Even we don't know what's happening."

"Oh, I hope nobody calls him, he'll be so upset. He's the kind of guy likes to *do* things, you know? It's like me up here, I want to *do* something, and it'd be even worse in a way for him." She pauses. "Well, in a way, anyhow. Not really. But you know how it is when you want to help somebody and you can't? Like when your kid gets sick?"

No; but Lila nods agreeably.

"I always hate that. Like when they've got a fever and you can't make them better? It's worst when they're babies and you know something's wrong because of how they're screaming, but they can't tell you what it is and it's just so fucking scary, right? You got kids?"

Lila shakes her head. Normally not having children is perfectly fine, but Sarah almost makes her feel guilty. Or inadequate. Missing a critical factor of today's panic and grief.

Sarah shrugs. "Lucky." She probably means Lila has less to let go of.

"How old are your children?"

"Twelve and nine. Boy and girl. Tim and Tiffany." She falters again, her eyes fill up. "My poor babies! What'll happen to them?" Again she grabs at Lila's arm. "Do you think they'd be okay? Without me? If that's what happens? What do you think?"

About whether they'd be okay without her, or whether that's what's going to happen? "Of course they'd be terribly upset. Naturally. But I'm sure they'd turn out fine in the end. Your husband sounds"—sounds what? Lila has no idea how he sounds—"like a nice man. Helpful."

"Yeah, he's okay." The changeable Sarah grins again. "Pisses me off. You know how long it took me to make him okay? And now maybe I won't end up getting much out of all that work."

"You must have married very young."

"I was eighteen. Knocked up. He was twenty. Boy"— she shakes her head—"that was a shitload of crap from my folks, and then getting used to each other and having kids so quick. I said right then, no more for a while, we need to get sorted out first. So we get sorted out and look what happens! You on your own?"

Lila shakes her head. "No, I'm with a friend." She never speaks of Tom to anyone but Nell and Patsy, but here, everything's different. "We were taking a holiday. Two weeks roaming around England, maybe a bit of Wales or Scotland. We've been planning for ages." How lovely this sounds; how remote.

"A guy or a woman friend?"

"A guy."

"Shit, that stinks. I bet you were really looking forward to it." They are edging closer to the washroom. Behind Lila, a short, elderly white woman has joined the line and, behind her, a Sikh man, turban knocked slightly sideways.

"I was. We were. We wanted to get away. Have some fun, see new sights." How tenderly she feels towards that man with whom she planned a holiday; if not towards the one who can't bear dying with her.

"You know, I've never been away just with Kevin. Not since the honeymoon, anyway, and that was only four days because we didn't hardly have any money. After that there's always been a kid around. Sometimes I've thought, if we could only get away, just the two of us, but it's kind of scary, too. Like, if we did, what would we do? We're so used to being with the kids, what if it was just us and we didn't have a clue?"

"Yes, I've wondered something along those lines, too."

"But you're not married to this guy?"

"No. He's married, I'm not."

"Oh." Sarah perceptibly closes up, draws away. Foolish Lila; what else would a married woman be likely to do? But at least Lila is now someone individual and interesting, and Sarah is regarding her with curiosity. "How does that work? Don't you mind? Does his wife know? Is it okay, me asking?"

Lila shrugs. "Sure." On the ground it wouldn't be okay at all, but on the ground there'd be a future and she would hardly be exchanging confidences with Sarah or anyone else. "Sometimes it's hard and doesn't work very well, and sometimes it's fine. And no, I don't imagine his wife knows, although who can say? I expect people often know things but don't want to admit them. To themselves, mainly. Too much disruption."

It's tricky, trying to discern just which one of them, Dorothy, Lila or Tom, is most lacking in courage. But Lila doesn't say that.

Sarah looks thoughtful. "I've wondered if I'd know if Kevin was screwing around. Oh, sorry, you probably don't like that, calling it screwing around. But that's what I'd call it, I guess because I'm a wife. I guess it depends which spot you're in, doesn't it?"

Lila thinks that's clever of Sarah. With her ability to distinguish varying points of view, she would be a good student of literature. "There are lots of words," Lila agrees. "You're right, it's a matter of perspective."

"I think I'd know." Sarah frowns. "But if he was, I don't know what I'd do. Kill him, likely, but then what? One thing, I wouldn't pretend I didn't know. Of course I can't keep my mouth shut about anything; sometimes Kevin says, 'For heaven's sake, Sarah, not everything's worth talking about.' But if you don't say things, how do you know what other people think? I'd just bust if Kevin was screwing around and I didn't say anything. I'd just bust open all over the kitchen floor like some big old watermelon."

She pauses, very briefly. "I wonder if Kevin'd get married again. If the worst happens. I guess he would." She sighs. "He's only thirty-two. And he'd want somebody for the kids, anyway. Man, that pisses me off. I'm going to haunt him if he does that. I wonder what that'd be like, haunting somebody. Seeing everything." She shivers. "Weird, thinking dead people might be able to do that. I sure wouldn't like it, somebody looking and listening all the time. Like, I wouldn't like some dead person doing that to me, but it'd be interesting to do it myself. Think of the secrets you'd know! Man, that'd be fun."

She looks cheerful now, and it's contagious. Lila finds herself wondering who she might haunt, whose secrets she might enjoy intruding on. Well, anyone, really. Not friends, necessarily, or loved ones. Strangers might even be preferable. Everyone has secrets, small and large privacies, and flitting from one to another would be an eternity of entertainment, far better than TV. She might start with Dorothy. Unless Tom got there first. That might overcrowd the room with inquiring spirits.

They could play a dire bedside spin on Dickens, with Lila appearing as ghost of lover past.

A small amusement.

"I wonder," Sarah says, "what does happen. Or if it's nothing at all." Lila, sobering, doesn't say what naturally leaps to mind, that they may find out very shortly. But of course the words are in the air.

The old woman behind Lila suddenly pipes up. How long has she been listening? "If you have faith," she says in a clear, quivering voice, "what happens is heavenly. Bliss and salvation. Joy we cannot imagine."

Lila has nothing to say to that. She is a little surprised that Sarah does, and in a voice turned instantly jeering and bitter. "Yeah? That'd be nice, all that joy. You'd think we'd be in a big rush to get there then, wouldn't you? But I don't see anybody praying for the damn plane to crash, do you? So that hardly makes any fucking sense, does it?" She is glaring at the woman.

What does it mean, Lila wonders, that up here, in this situation, outbreaks of affection aren't occurring at anything like the rate of rage?

Lips and eyes narrowed, Sarah turns back to her. Lila thinks she looks a little like a snake, and wouldn't be surprised to hear hissing. "I had a bellyful of that crap when I was a kid. Praise the Lord, my ass. More like, you do something bad, the Lord'll whip you silly. My folks went nuts when I got knocked up, said they'd pray for me but I'd have to repent or I'd be going to hell. Screw that. I told them Kevin and I'd be happy in hell, as long as they weren't there."

The old woman makes unhappy little throat sounds, but at least keeps quiet.

"You religious?"

A bit late to ask. Lila smiles. "No, but there's no telling what I may decide to believe by the end of the day." She may wind up crying "Jesus save me." Or, for that matter, "Hallelujah." She doubts it, but then, she has doubts about practically everything.

"I believe in my babies and Kevin. And me." Sarah's shakes her head, as if trying to dislodge some piece of knowledge. "Shit, this sucks. This really sucks." Lila could not agree more.

"I mean, you get up in the morning and you're all excited because you're going to be someplace totally different by the end of the day, and you run around trying to think of everything you need to remember and get everything taken care of—even food. You know, I made six dinners and froze them for everybody? Not for every night I'm gone, and Kevin can cook all right anyway, but just so at supper sometimes they'd be thinking about me? So I'd still be there in a way?

"And I was thinking about seeing my little sister for the first time in ages, and how much we have to talk about and how great it was going to be, showing her pictures of the kids and seeing where she lives and how she's changed, because she got away even farther than I did, and they pray for her too, I guess.

"So I mean, you're thinking about the place you're leaving and the place you're going to, but you forget to think about the part in the middle, and then it turns out to be the only thing that counts."

Lila must have thousands of words in her head, many of them capable of being combined in graceful forms to express with elegance various ideas, and here's skinny, freckled Sarah taking a very few, blunt words and saying pretty much the whole thing.

"How'd you figure what that guy was saying, that co-pilot?" Sarah asks. "Think he was telling us anything like the truth, or just trying to keep everybody quiet?"

"I don't know. I couldn't tell either. Both, maybe." How did Lila come to sound so prim? Five years of keeping an enormous secret may have done the trick. Not speaking about something important for such a long time may have robbed her of passionate speech.

There'd be a sorrow, a loss.

"Great voice, though, didn't you think?" Sarah looks mischievous. "Sexy. It'd be amazing, hearing that voice coming at you from the next pillow. Kevin's got a nice voice. I knew him all through school, and I remember when his voice changed, and then it kept getting deeper and deeper. I'm a sucker for voices. What's your guy's voice like?"

How can Lila describe something that has so many different tones for different purposes? "It's quiet most of the time. But he's a professor, like me, and he used to be a politician, and that's like acting: you make your voice project more and use it in different ways. In personal circumstances, too, so for instance you can tell another person how angry you are without having to raise your voice at all."

"Wow, you're a professor? What do you teach?"

"English literature, I'm afraid." As with the question of children, Lila feels oddly guilty. Insubstantial, by Sarah's standards.

"No shit. I used to love English in high school, it was my best subject. Sometimes I wish I had time to read, but having a job and the kids—well, if I did read, it wouldn't be anything good, likely. But maybe sometime. When the kids are grown up, in a few years. Oh." Her face tightens again.

"You'll be reading, don't worry. Picture yourself curled up in the evening with a book. Do you have a big comfortable chair? A fireplace?" Lila is trying to create a vision, a future.

"No fireplace. I'd like one, though. And I've always said, once the kids are grown up and gone we're going to get whole new furniture, because everything we've got's torn and stained. Well, it's not that bad, but you know kids. You can't keep things nice, and there's no point getting new stuff as long as they're roaring around."

It hurts to remember Lila's own house, where lamps lean over deep, soft chairs, and books can be cherished. Silence. Peace. Except for her heart floundering and flailing over matters to do with Tom; the past few years have been somewhat disruptive in that regard.

Still, just as in a book, the floundering and flailing contribute to plot. She and Tom may lack a common setting, and their characters may not, by some standards, bear very close scrutiny, but they do constitute a plot together.

How's he doing back there? She cannot, even arching on tiptoe, see past the bodies and heads in the way. "So," she turns back to Sarah, "you're travelling all on your own?" That would be lonely, she thinks. Her own journey may be difficult, but at least she has someone besides herself to take into account.

"Yeah. That's another reason I had to get out of my seat. The guy next to me was making me nuts. Scared me, too."

"Really? How?"

"Well, first he threw up, a couple of times. I hate that. I mean, I feel bad for people being sick, but I could hardly stand it with my own kids, never mind a complete stranger, and he didn't even say he was sorry or anything, just handed his barf bag to the flight attendant like he was returning a sandwich." Sarah giggles. "I guess he was, sort of.

"Then he had one of those squirter things, you know, for your breath? So after he's done throwing up he squirts his mouth and then he turns to me and says, can you believe this, he says, 'Well honey, I don't see much point in going down alone, do you? I think we could get to be good friends real quick, enjoy our last moments the best way we can. How about it?' No, wait, he said, 'How about it, babe?' Real cool. Really tempting." Sarah rolls her eyes.

"What did you say?" Lila understands how repulsive this must have been; but wouldn't it be nice if Tom had suggested enjoying his and Lila's last moments the best way they could?

"I told him to fuck off. He said, 'Oh come on, don't be like that, honey,' and I said, 'Christ, get a grip, don't be a total asshole; if you really think we're going to die, you want to die a total asshole?' And he got this real mean look. You know that squinty way guys get sometimes? I could kick myself, though, because that's when I decided to get up, and I went and said 'Excuse me' when I was leaving. I can't believe I excused myself to him, what a jerk. So anyway, if you want to get ahead of me in line, feel free, I'm not in any hurry to get back. Maybe I'll look around for someplace else to sit. Yeah, I better."

It's on the tip of Lila's tongue to suggest Sarah join her and Tom. The window seat is free, and it would be an act of kindness. How many acts of kindness could she rack up in her remaining moments? Enough so, in the event of there being a ledger somewhere, a last-minute rush of virtue could overwhelm her flaws and faults?

But. But there are some things, between her and Tom, and for herself. Some shifts to decipher. Sarah is lively and scared, and her presence would make it difficult to get very far. Wherever it is Lila desires to get. She'd like not to be angry, anyway.

Maybe later she can seek out Sarah and invite her to the window seat.

Later? What's the matter with her, is she an idiot?

She feels Sarah's hand on her arm. "You okay? You're not going to pass out or anything, are you?" She is looking at Lila anxiously. "You want to sit down?"

"Thanks, no, I'm fine." Sort of fine. Fine under the circumstances.

A grey-faced man emerges from a washroom, and Sarah's now at the head of the line. "Geez," she whispers, "seeing somebody that scared can make you more scared, don't you think?" Another door opens, and it's Sarah's turn. "Maybe I'll catch you later," she says. "Anyhow, it was nice meeting you." She laughs, shakes her head. "See? Just like we met over lunch or something. Isn't this weird?" And with a little wave, she is gone.

Lila immediately misses her.

She does actually need to pee now, and dodges quickly into the next free cubicle. What a relief! Also it's good, for a few minutes, to be alone, although in the absence of voices, the plane's engines are unnervingly loud. Should they sound so intrusive?

Sitting on the tiny toilet, manoeuvring around the tiny cubicle, washing her hands in the tiny sink, Lila wonders what it really might have been like, making love in this space. How uncomfortable and arousing it might have been, and what new positions might have been required.

Now she'll never know.

Oh. She'll never know.

She almost cracks her head on the sink, bending double. Sharp as knives, the shock of grief.

All the things she'll never know. She wants to put her arms around her brother, hang on tight. It's years since she has touched his skin, and they've known each other longer than anyone else in the world—they should at least have done that much. She should have had more lunches with Anne, and had Don and Anne's children, Lila's nieces and nephew, on more sleepovers and picnics and holidays. She has done some things, but never enough, and now there's so much that may be permanently undone.

She may never read another book, or enter another classroom or another argument. There may be no more belly laughter, or warm skin, or hot desire.

Patsy and Nell—every year they spend a week together, someplace with sunshine and water. They cook and drink and laugh and read, and sit with their bare feet propped on deck railings, talking over events and ideas, comparing the aging of throats and thighs, happily gluing their lives. And now Lila has blithely, thoughtlessly, flown out of their range.

She has so few places where she belongs; so few hearts with large spaces for her.

On a whim, she and Patsy once climbed a dim flight of stairs over a storefront to visit a palm reader. "You will be happy in love," the woman told Patsy, which cheered her although it turned out to be only temporarily true. She was happy until she and her husband Archie separated, more, it seemed, out of inadvertence than any bad act. "We forgot to pay attention," Patsy said. "I swear I wouldn't let that happen again." But another opportunity for love has not yet arisen for her.

"You will have a long life," the palm reader told Lila.

And love?

"Ah, there your hand is interesting. The line of affection disappears early. Very unusual," as if it were a matter for pride.

Perhaps the palm reader confused Patsy's hand with Lila's. Or muddled Lila's own life and love lines. In its various forms she has not felt deprived of love, or desperate, until now. But her life may not be long.

It's hard to stand up. Her fingers are white on the edge of the sink.

And out there in the cabin sits a man appalled that he's with her. She never imagined love was easy, but she didn't dream of this, either.

Oh no, that's her own voice whimpering. She is not a whimperer. She is not.

There is heart trouble in her family. Could she, like first her father, then years later her mother, be quietly, privately, having a heart attack? It hurts that much.

There is also heart trouble in her family in the form of oddly placed, or misplaced, affections. She may have fallen heir to that affliction, as well.

Lifting her eyes to the plain little mirror bolted over the sink, she sees her face, with all its middle-aged sags and lines and exaggerations, stiff and still with desire.

I want, she thinks.

She would have liked to see barrenness. Emptiness. A desert flat beyond horizons. She has an idea that she could see clearly there, and circumstances, desires and decisions would have perfectly pure, sharp edges.

This is perhaps where she is standing now: on the verge of extremes.

But everyone on this plane must be watching dreams flicker in the light of the fire; missed destinations. They all must have this much in common, much more than shared fate.

She stands quite still, now stopped not by grief, but by surprise: the dumbfounding sensation of her flawed heart growing large, inflating with astounding affection. Desire. A weird kind of happiness. What is this? A feeling, anyway, she would like to hold on to; one she could possibly bear to go down with.

seven

RADIANT, SHE STEPS OUT
of the washroom and back into chaos. Was she in there a
very long time? Some people regard her impatiently, as
if she's been holding them up. Elsewhere, others continue to cry out, in a range of tones, variations on, "Oh,
God, please." To Lila, the words now do not sound as
much like begging as like promising. "Let me try, give me
a chance," they plead, and then pledge, "I swear I'll do
better, and more."

Radiant, Lila has also stepped into the arms of the old
woman who was behind her in the line when she was
talking to Sarah. What's she doing, still waiting? "My
dear," she says, laying plump fingers on Lila's arm. What
happened to the shaken Sikh? In his place there's a balding, blond, muscled man, whom the old woman gestures
ahead. "You go on, I'd like a word with this young

woman." Nice, being called young; as if everything remains possible.

The old woman holding Lila's arm may be small and white-haired, and she may be wearing the sort of innocent, flowery print dress Lila's grandmother would have worn for, say, visiting June, but she also gleams with intention. She has made herself visible the way Lila can make herself large: with intensity, not size.

She has one of those old-lady bodies that slope downwards; a knoll of a body, a little foothill of a frame. She has the kind of body Lila could be heading towards, if Lila were heading towards any kind of old body. But what a glittering in the bright old-lady eyes.

"I couldn't help overhearing your conversation with the other young woman, and I've been waiting to speak with you. I'm very concerned for your soul."

Oh dear.

Still, how interesting fanaticism is. As well as tedious.

"My name's Adele Simpson, and I feel I simply must talk to you about how vital it is, the state of your soul. Especially now, when there may only be moments left for seeking redemption. Forgiveness for your sins. I don't suppose you want to hear, but today! All this! I cannot stay silent." Passion overtakes proper behaviour—fine. But why Lila and not the Sikh man who was surely, from Adele's point of view, even more distant from redemption?

Perhaps he was so distant he wasn't even on Adele's horizon.

Did she try this with Sarah? That would have been something to see. "The state of my soul," Lila says gently enough, "is my own concern, you know, not yours."

"Oh, no, it must be mine, too, do you see? I feel this day as a test and a judgment, I feel the Lord calling to our souls, and we must listen. We must!"

What if, as her last act, Lila believed she absolutely had to make some dim, uninterested student comprehend a poem, be enlightened by a phrase or saved by a particular sentence—might she not also be grasping at arms?

Something like that, anyway.

Adele doesn't look scared; intensity of purpose, putting salvation into words, may be her brand of hope. Possibly by now she is even scenting heaven, praying for the plane to go down. Possibly Lila's resistance is all that's preventing such a prayer. Such an outcome.

Adele's voice rises. "Don't you see, you must not die unredeemed and in sin. How can I make you see? Oh Lord, help me to do your work."

"Geez, lady." This is a young man, a boy, really, in jeans and black T-shirt and four golden earrings and one golden nose ring, now next in the line and shuffling impatiently. "You're in the way and you're ragging on people. Why don't you mind your own business? Go to the john or go pray for yourself, but what're you ragging on people for?" Ridiculous, but Lila's impulse is to protect Adele. Maybe it's the housedress, or the fervent eyes. If nothing else, fanatics get points for sincerity.

Evidently Adele, crisply gesturing him ahead while keeping her gaze and grip on Lila, needs no help. "Please listen. You must know the great wrong you are doing, you must, but you don't look like a bad woman; I'm sure you want to be good."

Extremities are one thing; simplicities quite another.

And what, exactly, do bad women look like? Odd, that some people still expect to see either evil or goodness as plainly as wrinkles or the colour of eyes.

"I thought if I spoke to you, that might be all you needed to change your life, that something must be waiting inside you for the word to be spoken. I'm sure, someone like you, you can't *want* to live in sin. Or die in sin. I couldn't pass by, do you see? I couldn't fail the Lord when it might be my last opportunity. How would I face Him at the gates of heaven, seeing you turned away and knowing a word from me might have made an eternal difference?"

Heavens, how eloquent the obsessed can be! It's a little worrying, that she almost makes sense. Well, not sense, but Lila can almost see that, from her point of view, Adele is doing exactly the right and necessary thing. "Thank you," Lila says carefully. "For your concern. I do see what you mean."

"Thank the Lord." Adele's face brightens. She looks almost sweet, almost jolly, nearly normal and harmless. "Now we can pray." The picture is comical, but Lila tries to swallow her laughter. "Don't worry, there's no need to get down on our knees, although of course that's always best. I find it harder myself these days, but the Lord doesn't mind. We can just hold hands and offer our prayers together. I know it's not easy to abandon pleasureful ways, or admit sins, or seek forgiveness. But I'm sure you also know that the greater the difficulty, the greater the reward. Oh, I'm so excited!" Indeed she must be.

"Now, hold my hand, dear, and we will pray." Shall pray, Lila thinks. There are differences between will and shall, which few people know any more. Or maybe, in this case, the emphatic "will" is exactly what Adele intends.

It's a lovely, round, happy face now. What a shame. "I respect your intentions," Lila says firmly, although respect is hardly the word, "and I know your belief is real to you, but if I prayed with you, I'd be lying, and of course you know how wrong that would be. Especially now." Adele looks as if Lila has hit her. Her face even reddens, as if struck by an actual blow. But then, like the optimist she apparently is, she revives.

"Oh dear, of course. I forgot that testimony is how I came to the Lord, and how you can, too."

This is like being in an unfamiliar country, or city, ignorant of local customs, having to pay close attention in order to catch rhythms of language and movement, to discern the unfamiliar and previously unknown. Interesting. Curious. On the other hand, Lila's been gone quite a while. Tom may be worried. She may be wasting extraordinarily precious time.

There is some small thing about Adele, though: not the business about salvation, repentance; more to do with virtue. A subject, no doubt, on Tom's mind, as well.

"You see, my dear, I was a sinner too, that's what I forgot for a moment, and I do apologize."

"Perfectly all right." Gosh, it's hard not to laugh. But that was a rather sharp glance Adele just shot Lila anyway.

The young man in the jeans, black T-shirt and golden rings here and there pauses briefly beside them, leaving the washroom. "She got to you, eh?" he says to Lila. He shakes his head, and all those rings, and edges past. He has, Lila notices this time, amazing eyes and cheekbones. How beautiful, despite garish camouflagings, some young men can be.

Adele also watches him, although with a different view. "I must find him later. I can see his longing, too." She's going to be busy if she plans on converting passengers one at a time. And some of them will be a good deal more irritable about it than Lila.

"You see," Adele resumes, "I couldn't understand for a very long time why so much went wrong in my life." Uh-oh. So that's what "testimony" means. "I thought I was a good enough person, and I couldn't imagine I deserved some of the things that happened to me. But I was swept up by a physical desire when I was very young. How could I know?" Adele looks to Lila for understanding, or maybe for forgiveness, although that's ludicrous, all things considered.

"I married a good-looking man who drank and blackened my eyes and hurt me in many other ways as well. We had a son. I wanted so much that he not be like his father, and that he learn to be good and kind, as I believed I was. I gave him every morsel of love and attention I had, and I was so sure he would be different.

"When he grew up," Adele has tears now in her cast-down eyes—but how many times, if this is her usual "testimony," must she have told this story?—"he came to me and told me he lay down with men. He wanted me to meet the man he was living with. He said we were all his family. I couldn't believe it. I couldn't bear it. All those years I loved him, and then never to see him again."

"What?" Lila must have missed something; there seems to be a large gap in the tale. "Did something happen to him?"

Adele looks irritated. A rather impatient evangelist, it seems. "I said: he lay with men. And that idea of his, being a family, it was disgusting. I said to him, 'How could you do this to me?' I begged him to change. I said I would forgive him if he'd only change, but if he wouldn't, he wasn't my son. After all those years, suddenly the person sitting at my kitchen table wasn't my son. He left. I didn't miss him exactly, since he was no longer my son, but I mourned my little boy."

Lila shivers.

"And I asked God, too, 'How could You do this to me? All of it, my husband, the boy—what did I do to deserve such troubles?' For the longest time, I couldn't hear an answer. Then I went to one particular church and found people to talk to, to ask about these things, and do you know what they said?"

Lila shakes her head. It's beyond her.

"They told me God must love me very much. That He gives special burdens to those who are strong enough, and even though I didn't know I had a great longing for Him, He knew, and these trials He sent were intended to bring me to Him. So you see, I had sinned by my attention to earthly matters, and He took them away and showed me the true path."

Adele smiles happily up at Lila. "He can do the same for you, it's not too late, and it's so terribly important. The wrong kind of love, that's what it is. That's what I learned, and I was saved."

"I see." Lila nods. It's hard to think of what else to say. "Do you wonder about your son? Do you know how he is?"

"Oh, heavens, all that was twenty-five years ago; he could be anywhere. I suppose these days, he might be dead." How content she sounds. "We've never heard from him again. My husband tried to tell me what happened was my fault. He simply hates my faith. I wish I could have saved him, but he's been so angry, so"—Adele shrugs—"I have to go on, knowing it's only another test on the road to eternal glory. That gives me such joy!" She beams even harder.

She is completely nuts.

Imagine seeing other people's lives merely as hurdles for her own salvation. Imagine being so distant from heartbreak and brutality, her son's or her husband's, not to mention her own, that she tucks them away as God's will.

"That's quite a god you have there," Lila says.

"Oh yes, indeed, exactly. I'm so glad you see that."

"And do you see me as another test of your faith?"

Adele's forehead crinkles. "Yes, I suppose, in a way. It's never been easy for me to approach strangers, although I've had to many times; it's part of what we do. I always have to make myself strong enough by saying it's what God wants. Sometimes it can even be frightening, because people don't always know what they need, and they aren't always ready to hear. They can be angry, but then I think, really they're just frightened by the truth. Facing up to God's judgment is hard. But of course when I heard you speaking with that other young woman, I knew there was no choice. It's a God-given opportunity, do you see? You have a chance for repentance, and if the worst happens you're saved just in time, and if it doesn't, your life takes a new path anyway, and you're separated from sin."

Interesting concept, being separated from sin. Like a fence, with sin on one side, Lila on the other. She pictures herself scrambling over in fairly short order.

A peculiar word, too: sin. She understands good and bad in quite a different way. Good is respect, care and affection—what her grandmother and Aunt June called decency, mainly. And bad is the opposite. Simple enough.

Lila's mother and father were bad, together, because they lacked respect, care and affection for each other. Their bad act was staying together. Tom and Dorothy, also, may be bad in a similar way, although that's an assumption; Lila doesn't know enough about their life together to be entirely certain. Lila and Tom, on the other hand, have generally, with the critical exception of recent moments and a few others along the way, been good.

This is not, however simple, a perspective Lila will undertake to explain to Adele. They are unlikely to have a meeting of the minds.

"Your husband?" she asks. "You stayed with him?"

"Goodness yes. Of course. It hasn't been easy, but the Lord gives me courage. Remember, marriage vows are really vows to God, not man. I'd like to talk to your friend; he needs to be reminded as well." Wouldn't Tom be pleased if Lila returned with Adele in tow; wouldn't he enjoy a natter about the divine importance of marriage vows? That would be a really good punishment.

"I'll remind him, don't worry."

"You will? Then you do understand?" How hopeful she looks. And also rather stupid, and also rather evil.

"Oh yes. I understand."

"I'm so happy. I feel as if, if this plane goes down, my last acts will have demonstrated my faith. I'm very grateful. I hope you are, too?"

"Definitely. Grateful." The idea of madness—of going mad—has occasionally crossed Lila's mind as something that could be, assuming one survived it, a broadening, enlightening sort of experience. New perceptions from new perspectives, casting entirely fresh light, the whole world altered and tilted.

Maybe so, if one had an invigorating sort of madness, but there are awful alternatives; including Adele's sort, which looks like deliberate dimming of human light, not expansive at all, and also quite vicious.

"It's been—interesting to meet you, Adele. Good luck." Luck can have no meaning to her. Luck, good or bad, will be simply God's will.

What unhappy luck for Lila to run into her instead of, oh, a zen monk smiling plumply at foolish attachments.

Satori, yes; salvation, no. Lila laughs, causing a few people to stare again.

Now Adele can wander the plane, giving her testimony, saving last-minute souls in the obsessed, self-absorbed style of the ancient mariner. That should keep her occupied and distracted from doom, which seems to be the general point of her faith. Heavens, what a life!

Yes, well, what a life Lila has, herself.

Where does lying fall in her personal scheme of goodness and badness? Where is the breaking of promises on her scale of decency? She is, if not a liar or promise-breaker herself, at least a very serious accessory.

She shrugs, joggling a man pushing by. It would have

been better for her parents to discard their promise to each other than to endure their lonely years together. There *is* a scale of decency, in which actions must be weighed against each other. Lila is as certain of that as Adele is of redemption.

Lies are more slippery. There are kind or weary lies, such as the ones she and Tom may occasionally tell each other. There are words left unsaid which result in quite false impressions. And there are big, blatant lies for which the most sinuous reasoning can't give a good account.

Those are the ones, difficult to arrange on her scale of decency, in which Lila is implicated.

This is neither new nor soluble. She shrugs again.

What happened to radiance?

Still there. Or some similar, glittering, peculiar sensation.

Adrift from Adele, returning to Tom, Lila feels nearly insubstantial, unreal. She is floating. Her feet stepping along the aisle don't seem to touch it. Her head is light. She has no idea what will happen when she gets back to her seat, but if any day were going to slice into her heart and open it up, today would. Maybe, if she looked again, it would break.

She bends, peers out the nearest window.

Oh.

Flames still flicker orange even in the high sunlight. The shadow of the plane on the clouds below reflects the fire darkly. Has it spread? Is it larger, smaller, more contained or more extensive than before? Tom could gauge. He saw it first, watched longer, and perhaps has spent the time she's been away looking out at it.

"Please get back to your seat, ma'am." Sheila has stopped in front of her. "You mustn't stand in the aisles." Her make-up isn't what it once was, but she has managed to tuck in her blouse. Lila looks carefully into her eyes, but still can't decipher what they're hiding: good news or bad.

"Is there," she hears herself asking, "anything I can do?" What, clean up vomit? Urge other people back to their seats?

"Thank you, but the best thing to help is to go back to your seat. And please don't forget to fasten your seat-belt." Sheila is wearing the glazed, calming smile of the professional dealing with the annoying.

"Are we . . . ?" Lila begins. She won't finish the question, although she knows what she's asking.

So does Sheila. "We'll hear from the pilots whenever there's anything. Any updates. I'm sure it'll be soon. Meanwhile, please, ma'am." She is looking over Lila's shoulder. Of course she must be in a hurry, much to do, much to accomplish, many needs to attend to.

"Hey, hi there." The many-ringed young man from the washroom line-up is leaning, glittering in his own way, into the aisle, looking up at her. "You finally got away from the Bible babe, huh? Sorry I couldn't help you better." He's grinning like a conspirator. And why not? She smiles back.

"Thanks for the effort, anyhow." He's not quite as young as she'd thought, but he does have those gorgeous brown eyes and sculpted cheekbones, although the cropped dark hair is, to Lila's taste, unfortunate. From here she can see Tom, a few rows ahead, bent forward slightly, right arm moving. What is he doing?

He's apparently not, at any rate, anxiously wondering where she's gotten to and if she's all right. The young man with the eyes and cheekbones and rings is still smiling up at her.

"Actually," she tells him, "she was interesting in an awful sort of way. You might want to know that she mentioned hunting you down. She thinks your soul could use some saving, also."

It does feel a bit cruel to make fun of crazy, insistent Adele. This wouldn't be a nice time for the plane to go down, not a nice last moment at all.

"Christ, that's all I need. Listen, if I shift over, would you sit down for a few minutes? Keep me company, ward her off?" He's already unbuckling, moving towards the empty seat beside him.

He is quite beautiful.

"Maybe for a minute. I don't think I'd be much help if she's as determined as she was with me, though. Are you on your own?"

"No, but my girlfriend's gone to the can. We were kind of getting on each other's nerves so we took turns taking a break. You?"

"No. My seat's just up there," and she nods towards Tom.

"The dude that's writing?" Is that what he's doing? She peers, and it does look as if he's scratching away at something on his lap. "I spotted him when I came back and sat down. I thought, There's a pretty cool guy. Shit." He shakes his head. "Hey, I'm Jim Webster." He reaches out to shake her hand. "Friends call me The Web."

"Goodness, do they? I'm Lila. Friends call me Lila."

This is ridiculous. What is she doing here, sidetracked by glorious bones, deep eyes and golden rings? Do they hurt? Especially the one in his nose?

And what is Tom writing?

There's an abrupt crackling. "Ladies and gentlemen"—that cool, deep voice again—"could I have your attention." Instantly, except for the sound of the plane itself, the cabin is almost silent. The Web grasps Lila's hand as if she is his last touch of skin.

"Oh god," he moans. Poor kid is terrified. He could be one of her students. He could, if she had ever especially felt the desire, have been one of her children. She would like to moan, too, and almost gets up to go to Tom, but this boy—this scared man—how can she?

The tug of the vulnerable young is not resistible. Which she supposes is what Tom keeps telling her. Apparently, like his well-launched, grown-up daughters, it doesn't matter how old the vulnerable young become.

There's a joke about that, although Tom, when she told it to him, did not find it funny: A couple in their nineties go to a lawyer, seeking divorce. The lawyer is astounded that this tottery pair, obviously on their last legs, are determined to separate. "At this point," he asks, "why would you bother? What took you so long?"

"Well," they tell him, "we had to wait for the children to die."

Where is The Web's girlfriend? Why isn't he looking around for her, trying to get to her, or why isn't she reaching for him?

Lila sees Tom isn't looking around, either.

Possibly none of this matters. Everyone here, except maybe those with small children, must be alone in their souls at this moment. Lila settles back and lets her hand be gripped.

"Thank you. This is your co-pilot, Frank McLean, again. As I promised earlier, we intend to bring you up to date on developments and to respond to some of the questions you've been raising. First, many of you have noticed some changes in air pressure."

Does that account for the headache beginning to build behind Lila's eyes? Sometimes she's wondered what it would be like to go blind; to have words blur and fade, losing meaning in front of her eyes. It would start small, with a pain much like this one.

God, fate, karma—whatever—often seems quite a joker, popping up with whatever cruel trick a person most fears, whatever hurts worst. Or, an alternative prank, sneaking up with the most startling, unexpected variation of doom. Like today. Either way, what a laugh for the heavens.

"While we regret the discomfort you may be experiencing, we want to reassure you that the air is fully safe and adequate. Those of you travelling with very small children or those of you with chronic ear problems should be aware, however, that there may be some minor risks. Your flight attendants will be able to advise you of appropriate precautions you may want to take." Somewhere a woman, no doubt one with a small child, cries out briefly.

"As to our main problem"—and how many are there exactly, beyond painful pressure and flickering wings?— "to this point, we have been unable to gain manual control of the wings' fire-extinguishing system, which is not operating automatically as it should. Naturally, those efforts continue, with the help of communications with experts at ground control and the aircraft manufacturer, and we have every expectation of success."

Isn't life just one thing after another? First the fire, bad enough, but then the extinguisher system fails. Human bodies can also fall apart this way. A single insignificant trouble seeps into arteries, plugging them, or slips into organs, causing them to collapse. Few people know when this is happening. They find out in cataclysmic ways, and may well not connect disaster with the original small flaw.

This can be true in other matters, as well. It's not always simple to distinguish the trivial from the vital in much of day-to-day life, and this may result in larger confusions and blunders. Tom mentions a movie he and Dorothy have seen, telling Lila the plot, his impressions, and weeks down the road, one night when he's leaving

Lila for home, she snaps that they never have enough time, he never makes enough time, and he says for god's sake, he does his best, and off they go until they are finally left staring at each other angry and baffled, and with no idea that this started with a plot he'd described from a movie he saw with his wife.

"Due to this function delay, however, we are now flying on three engines." There are gasps, but how can anyone be surprised? Lila is surprised they still have three—and for how long will they?

The Web is taking deep, harsh breaths. "In fact," the voice continues warmly, reassuringly, "we've been flying on three engines for approximately the past eight minutes, so you can judge for yourselves that there is only a marginal difference." Lila sees heads nodding; oh, they agree, they agree, scarcely a difference at all—what a relief!

Don't get your hopes up, she thinks. Take a look out the window.

"We have remained in constant contact with our departure and various possible arrival locations, and have been proud to be able to reassure everyone that you are responding to our difficulties with calm and dignity." The Web moans again, but others, still nodding, now also look pleased with themselves. Lila wonders if this clever speech was carefully crafted long ago and goes everywhere on these planes on a set of fill-in-the-problem, reassure-the-passengers cards. Either that, or this Frank McLean is unusually coherent, a shrewd psychologist of the air.

She hopes the pilot is as good at keeping them flying as his co-pilot is at this small chore. Perhaps they flipped coins: "Heads you keep them quiet, tails you try to fly this fucker." She imagines them hooting, and slapping their thighs.

"In consultation with ground experts, we have had to make a series of decisions, among other things, settling on a destination." Lila suspects their destination is obvious, but maybe she's wrong. She also thinks he's still using far too many words—a sign that succinct, blunt fact would not be bearable?

"To bring you up to date, we determined from the start that we were beyond a feasible return to a North American airport. Ordinarily"—ordinarily!—"in that situation we would, as I mentioned earlier, consider Iceland. However, due to electrical storms in that region, we have ruled it out, and in fact have concluded that Heathrow remains our optimum preference. We are now following a revised flight plan that is actually slightly more direct than our usual one. Also, naturally, we will have priority landing rights, so I am pleased to announce, ladies and gentlemen, that if all goes as expected, we should arrive approximately ten minutes ahead of our originally scheduled landing."

He sounds so cheerful and confident about this that Lila imagines some passengers may be happily anticipating time for an extra drink at the airport, or an early arrival at a rendezvous.

"We are now flying somewhat south of our normal route over the Atlantic." There is a fresh stirring of unease at this reminder that they are over water. Lila feels it herself, the horror of falling into that cold expanse, sinking irretrievably into a world of strange, unknown creatures, her flesh becoming food for their flesh. She still can't think exactly why this seems worse than plunging into hard, unforgiving earth. The result for passengers is the same, after all, and certainly from the point of view of people going about their business on the ground, it's far preferable. Imagine this huge craft suddenly appearing over land, plummeting through the clouds, wiping out lives instantly vulnerable due to an accident of geography and where they happen to be standing.

There are perilous prospects ahead for various unsuspecting English people. Look out Cornwall, for instance, those quaint little resorts, all the bed-and-breakfasts. Oh, look up, look up!

"We will also be shifting to a lower altitude. In fact you can probably feel this already occurring." Thank heavens he said that. Otherwise Lila would have sworn they were beginning a slow plunge.

Maybe they are, and he's trying to keep people quiet as long as he can.

Oh, those last moments, heading straight down, terrible seconds! Such turmoil, people scrambling and hurtling about—it's Lila's turn to grasp The Web's hand very hard.

"Again, we're asking everyone to remain in your seats at all times except to use the washrooms. Along with changing our altitude, we anticipate some manoeuvres intended to compensate for any losses of power we experience, and we want to ensure that no passengers or crew are injured during these exercises." Exercises? Strenuous, hearty, mechanical aerobics that will leave the plane and its passengers more fit at the end?

But okay, maybe that's true. If they do survive, Lila can't imagine who wouldn't be permanently changed in some regard, possibly made stronger.

"Therefore, don't be alarmed by any unexpected movements of the aircraft. We will not be able to forewarn you when some manoeuvres are being attempted, but you should be perfectly safe with your seatbelts fastened. Those of you travelling with children should take particular care to ensure they are well secured.

"Again, your flight attendants are available to provide assistance. We regret the delay in bringing today's in-flight movie to you, but the attendants will shortly be asking you to lower your window blinds and it will begin. If there are further matters about which you need to be advised, we will briefly interrupt the movie.

"Finally, as many of you no doubt know, both this airline and this aircraft have excellent safety records. It is virtually unknown for a plane of this type to experience any sort of crisis that warrants serious alarm." That sounded like a flat-out lie; possibly because there already is serious alarm.

"Thank you for your patience." His voice vanishes with a click and once again the cockpit is its own world, where perhaps Frank McLean and Luke Thomas are handing each other high-fives, made mirthful by their hoax, and by hopelessness.

Somewhere towards the end of the speech, maybe when he mentioned the movie, Lila got furious again. Surely they deserve to be told what it means that a wing is on fire. Surely people are owed the right to prepare their hearts for final moments, if that is a possibility at all. It's one thing for that silk-voiced man and his friend—at least she hopes they're not enemies—to have their hands on the controls of the sound system, and on the controls of the plane. But in no way do their hands belong on people's final moments.

And everyone is supposed to obediently lower blinds and watch a Western, however cleverly nouveau? Pulling down blinds hardly puts out the fire, does it? It doesn't go away just because people can't see it.

There are lots of things Lila doesn't look at directly, but they go on anyway. She can scarcely bear to imagine Tom at home and tries very hard not to, but that doesn't mean that isn't exactly where he is: enjoying his fireplace on winter nights, building and fixing this and that (although he claims to be clumsy and unskilled around the house), reading bits of interesting books and articles out loud, sitting in his room of memories admiring his life, lying in his bed, reaching out on occasion, no doubt, touching skin.

Lila can close her eyes like blinds, but sometimes bitter images blaze through her lids anyway.

This is not the time. There is no time.

"I could just spit," she tells The Web.

"I can tell. You're busting my hand." But he's smiling. Still, a bit unfair, when she didn't complain at him hanging so hard onto her. "How come you're mad?"

She sighs. "I don't know, really. The business about the movie, I think."

"Yeah. I wish it wasn't an oater. I sure don't want to go down watching the back end of a horse." It's a joke, or a brave stab at one, but he's made himself go pale. "Aren't you scared?"

"Sure. Of course. Only, sometimes being scared makes me angry. Because anger feels better, I guess. It doesn't seem as helpless as fear, although"—she sighs again—"I suppose it probably is."

"Yeah?" He looks interested, and as a result less afraid. "My girlfriend's sort of like that. She goes off the deep end real easy; she says it's better to be mad than sad. That what you mean? Is it some kind of female thing?"

Lila laughs. "It does ring a bell, I admit. What does she get mad about?"

"Me. Our folks. Her job. And she's totally pissed about all this." When he gestures, Lila sees that the hand she was holding so tightly is tattooed with what looks like a pink peony surrounded by a cluster of green leaves. That can't be right; who'd have a peony tattooed on his hand?

A rosebud on the butt, maybe. Years ago, Lila considered getting one herself, just for the hell of it, because she was tickled by the idea of something privately pretty, but she never got around to it.

This could almost make her weep.

She had no idea she was such a fool.

"Where were—are—you going?" This is a question she failed to ask Adele, whom she imagines headed for some evangelical rally, an international gathering of button-holing, arm-clutching, redemptive, tragic wackos. Wouldn't that be something to see! Hundreds of muted print housedresses, and dark suits, plain ties, white shirts, all the blissful faces, every one stoned on salvation. Do people like that have theological schisms? Lila bets that if they do, they must be quite fierce and tiny.

"We were going to bum around for a month. Get our-selves together, you know?" Lila does. "Her folks don't like me and mine can't stand her and it's not like we have to care but it gets on our nerves." He snorts. "Man, who knew about nerves! This is really bad. How about you?"

"The same. My friend and I were going to wander around like you for a couple of weeks. We have family problems as well." And there'll be more when this is over. What the hell is Tom doing? Craning, she can just glimpse him sucking on a pen. Funny, to be the one avoiding cru-cial conversations, when usually she's the one who starts them.

Don't get sad, get mad. She'd like to meet The Web's girlfriend.

"Do I have to call you The Web?" she asks. "It makes me feel as if I'm sitting with Spiderman."

He shrugs. "No. My girlfriend calls me Jimmy. It's my buddies call me The Web." He grins. "Except when we're at her folks' house, then she calls me The Web, too, because it gets them crazy. And the tattoos and the motorcycle, and they think I'm too old for school. I dropped out of high school and now I'm going back to learn computers. I figure that's the way of the future, right? The thing to get into?"

"It certainly sounds like it." Literature, either the learning or the teaching of it, is not, in the view of many experts or for that matter of many students, the way of the future. Which may in any case be straight down.

"Yeah. So it's a one-year course, and we figure this is our last chance to get away together. Figure out where we're going, maybe decide to get married, I don't know. We had to go on the cheap, but that didn't hardly matter. Shit."

Lila pats his hand. Under the peony, or whatever the hell it is, it's a strong, tense, young hand. Rather an appealing hand. She pats it again.

"I drive delivery for a drugstore, and Mel's in a pizza joint, cooking mostly, but it's not so cool any more. We aren't either of us stupid or anything, it's just, in school we could take off on my Harley and ride all over the place, and that's what we really wanted to do, so we quit school so we could keep the bike in shape and have money to keep going. You ride?"

Lila shakes her head. "I'd like to, though." Suddenly she would, she would. To her surprise, she finds she longs to dress in leather and roll along highways, skin burning from air and speed, low to the ground and exposed. She hasn't thought of this before, but now it's another enormous lost desire to be mourned.

"Too bad. You've really missed something. At least, we're crazy about it. But you can't go forever on minimum wage, taking orders and crap. Anyhow, we might want to have kids, and"—he grins—"they'll need their own bikes. So that's why I'm going back to school. I figure if I can fix bikes, computers shouldn't be that much harder, right? Which is okay for me, but Mel has to keep making pizzas till we work out something better.

Anyhow, when we get back we're moving in together, see how that goes."

He stops, then mutters, again, "Shit."

"I know." Lila tries to sound comforting, at least.

He is telling all this as if he's storing it in one of the computers he's been hoping to study. Like Sarah, like Lila for that matter, he seems to feel putting his story into the mind of a stranger will keep him alive in some form. Or like others, he is drowning out the sounds of terror in his own ears.

Jimmy's life, however he has adorned and decorated it, isn't especially unusual, but equally it is, of course, unique. There are dozens and scores of stories here. Like Adele, Lila could go from row to row, seat to seat, grasping arms. Instead of offering salvation, she would demand to hear tales of all these lives.

"You ever hated somebody your kids go out with?"

So much for cheekbones and eyes—naturally he only sees someone maternal in Lila's bones and flesh. But what was she thinking? Surely not something else, not *that* kind of story.

"I don't have kids." Tom does, though, and has spoken of a couple of completely unsuitable young men, in his view, linked to one or the other of his daughters now and then. "You have to ride it out," he's said. "If you crack down, it gets worse. What I did was kill the pricks with kindness; that took the shine off."

"But," Lila goes on, "I understand it's smart to pretend to like your kids' choices, whether you do or not. Or at least be polite. Otherwise people get their backs up and hang on whether they actually want to or not." Was that tactless?

"Yeah, I hope I'm that smart when we have kids. Her folks think I'm a loser and mine think she's, I dunno, a slut or something, so I guess that makes us tighter. Not," he adds quickly, "that we wouldn't be tight anyway. But we know we gotta look after each other, too."

"That's nice. Looking after each other."

"Except, you know, it's tough today, for sure. That's why we took turns hitting the can, to get away for a few minutes, calm down. You know how people get on your nerves sometimes, just little things?" Lila nods; she does. "Mel's real hyper anyway, and her legs were bouncing like she was running and it was making me nuts. So she got mad and said at least she should be able to be scared her own way."

Good for her.

"How long have you been together?"

"Ten years, almost. Since she was twelve and I was fourteen, except for breaking up sometimes when we'd have a fight or want to go out with somebody else. Even so, we always get back. Like, it's not like I don't know she'll be back and she knows I'll be sitting here." He looks abruptly sad. "At least if we go down, we're going together. You feel like that? With the guy you're with?"

One of the things Lila likes very much about many young men these days is that they know how to ask questions. It seems to her their worlds are bigger than those of older men, including Tom sometimes, who grew up talking about themselves and never stopped.

"The thought crossed my mind," she tells Jimmy cautiously. "That if this were going to happen, I was glad he and I were together." She takes note, silently, of her own past tense.

Jimmy and his friend appear to take better account of each other than Tom and Lila do; but then, they've been together much longer than Tom and Lila, who could be their parents. She sighs. "I should get back to him."

"Yeah, I guess. He's probably wondering." Not noticeably.

Jimmy looks a bit bereft. Lila pats his slim, flamboyant hand once more. "Your girlfriend will be back any minute."

"I just hope the Bible babe doesn't get here first, that's all. Thanks for the company. It was nice of you. It was nice meeting you."

"You too. You'll be fine. We'll be fine."

She has no faith in that at all, and it sounded as if she were speaking to a child. Nevertheless. Leaning over, she kisses him lightly on the high arch of his cheekbone. "Thanks, Jimmy." For, she supposes, giving her heart. A little hope for love, a good example.

"Hey!" comes an outraged voice from over Lila's shoulder. "What the fuck are you doing?"

"Chill, Mel," Jimmy orders.

"Chill, shit. I go away for a few minutes and you got some old broad snuggled up kissing you? Chill yourself, asshole."

If this is Jimmy's girlfriend, Lila feels some sympathy with his parents. Or hers. Or all parents everywhere. She rises with, she hopes, some dignity. Old broad!

Although apparently a threatening one, even to this exotic young woman. Narrow, amazingly vivid, she's a jungle orchid, something wild. Her large dark eyes are outlined in black, cheeks splashed with colour, wide lips painted a deep red. Black hair falls below her waist, and she's wearing a bright blue, bright green outfit that looks like what cyclists wear on the road. Look at her bones!

If these two, Jimmy and Mel, ever had children together, they'd be stunning.

People do not, as a rule, much resemble what they do for a living, but it's hard to imagine this woman stooped over pizza ovens.

"I'm Lila," reaching out her hand—who invented hand-shaking? It's a very disarming sort of gesture, anyway, which is likely its point—"and I have no designs on Jimmy."

Mel looks embarrassed, drops her eyes. "Sorry. I'm Mel. Melissa. I'm kind of uptight."

"Me too. It's like a twelve-step program, isn't it? My name is Lila and I'm kind of uptight. Uptights Anonymous?"

When Mel laughs, Lila sees what must appeal to Jimmy: an earthy young woman who can't contain herself. She is spilling out of herself; maybe she always does, not only today.

Imagine being that sort of person.

If Lila were creating herself again, she would pay utter attention. She would perform even the smallest act intently. She would be electric. She would make her own hair stand on end.

"Lila," Jimmy offers, "was keeping me company and saving me from this Bible-thumper we met in the line to the john. She got Lila, and she was coming after me. Hey, babe, you've been a while."

Mel shrugs. Her shoulders go very high and very low inside the skin of her outfit. "I met some people, too. Then when the announcement came on, nobody moved, everybody wanted to hear. Except nobody still knows. Do they?" she asks Lila, flinging herself into the seat Lila just vacated.

She's wearing low green leather boots. When she sits, her belly stays flat, doesn't ripple out like Lila's. She is very beautiful. Since Lila never was, even at Mel's age, this is not envy, but appreciation of a striking piece of art.

Mel has a tattoo, a match to Jimmy's, on her own left hand. "This?" she says, seeing Lila notice and waving it closer. "We got matching flowers, like, we think engagement rings are junky, so we got matching tattoos."

"What kind of flowers are they?" Because to Lila they

still look like peonies, florid and unlikely, not to mention in real life susceptible to ants.

Mel shrugs. "No kind, I guess. We never asked. We just wanted something that showed. Man it hurt, getting it on the hand. Means"—she grins—"we can't leave each other, though. Not after you go through that. It's just about the most amount of pain I ever had."

Her face changes radically. She looks like a little girl, although an untamed, contrary one. "If we crash, do you think it'll hurt much?"

"I don't think so. If it happens, I think it'll be too fast for that. Maybe for a second or so, but that's it, I'm sure." Lila doesn't believe that at all.

Mel nods. "I hope so. We'd die, though, right?" Jimmy has taken her other hand, the one nearest him, and is stroking it with his fingers, green-petalled at their base.

"I expect so." How is Lila supposed to know? It must be that to these two, she could be a mother. She can see it's a role one could grow into, a presumption of wisdom, causing the head to swell. Gratifying and tempting, although also, since she has no view of herself as a mother, slightly dismaying. She could use a mother, or someone, herself.

"Good," Mel says, satisfied. "I couldn't stand living if I was going to be all bashed up and busted. I'd really hate that."

Funny, that possibility hadn't occurred to Lila. But what if they do get all the way but then crash low, trying to land—she might just be badly broken. Then what? Pain, paralysis perhaps, twisted limbs and organs, and who would care for her?

She should have had children. They might not have liked to, but they would have had to oblige.

No they wouldn't, what was she thinking? Children turn their backs on parents all the time, and so they should. Look at Jimmy and Mel, look at Tom's daughters, look at herself, for that matter. She did not kick over her job or her life to go and help care for her father during his last illness. She visited as often as she could, driving the few hundred kilometres there and back as his heart surged and collapsed through three attacks before the final one; but she did not stay long. She sat beside his bed in the hospital and held his hand, and they smiled at each other, but their habit of benevolent silence felt, by then, unbreakable and necessary.

She could not stay there with him and her mother. She felt choked, and drove away gasping for air.

When he died, her mother phoned to tell her. When her mother died, the neighbour who found her body called.

In her turn, Lila would also be alone. You can't expect even friends like Patsy or Nell to take on onerous care; that's not the sort of thing that's assumed, presumed, of friendship. She has imagined getting old on her own, trying to look after herself, and finally failing. She just didn't imagine it happening soon.

Dorothy would look after Tom. It's what spouses surely do, locked together no matter what. It's what Lila's mother did, as best she could.

If Lila were maimed and Tom were not, he would not look after her. That's a terrible difference: he would look after Dorothy in such a circumstance, but would have to abandon Lila.

Son of a bitch. Not his fault, but son of a bitch anyway.

If Tom were maimed and Lila were not, she would never get near him. Because how would they explain her attention, her devotion? How very odd, Dorothy would naturally think.

These are the kinds of things Lila and Tom know, but only remotely. Well, today's the day, isn't it?

"You okay?" Jimmy asks.

"Sorry," says Mel, "I didn't mean to upset you."

"It's okay." They're nice, noticing kids, tattoos, rings, spandex and all. "I just had one of those shocks. Reality kicking in."

Mel nods. "Yeah, it's hard to keep knowing all the time."

"It certainly is." She smiles. "Now I'd better get back to my companion, I've been gone long enough." Enough? For that matter, companion? Are she and Tom companions? She would have thought so, and they've even said so often enough, but true companions look after each other, and she has clearly seen that they would not.

Already Jimmy and Mel are shifting back to each other, a psychic alteration that binds them, excludes the rest. Also Mel's left leg is beginning to jiggle, and her fingers twine nervously with Jimmy's.

Lila would love her students, if she could be with them again. She would care passionately for the dullest of them. She would embrace the most vicious, or dim, of her colleagues. She would love the light streaking through the windows of her office, slashing its walls. She would leave her door open and be grateful for the raucous traffic outside, all those people tramping firm wooden floors.

She would be more urgently attentive to Patsy and Nell, who have their own troubles. She would speak with more passion than ever about the importance of beautiful words, and would use her own words better to say what she means and what she desires. She would spring loose, leap free, every which way.

She would touch fabrics, taste foods, see shapes and colours in eternally grateful and observant ways. She would plant her feet on the earth and never lift them again.

She wouldn't miss a thing.

She would try to love with a full, unequivocal heart, and sink and swim in the soothing equivalent joy. She would touch Tom's skin as if it is a miracle; which after all it has been.

Coming up behind him, she touches his busy shoulder.

eight

....

HE LOOKS UP, STARTLED.
"Oh," he says, grabbing at papers. "You're back." He shuffles sheets together and stands to let her past.

She intends to do her best. "Sorry I was so long. There was that line-up, and then I kept meeting people. You okay? What've you been doing?"

He seems uneasy, embarrassed, even guilty, as if he's had a quick fling in her absence. "Writing," he mutters.

"What?"

"Writing," he repeats, more clearly.

"Yes, but what?"

"A letter."

Oh. To those left behind.

"I know it sounds stupid."

Lila wouldn't say it sounds stupid, exactly.

So much for fine intentions, so much for full, unequivocal hearts. She could just burst—how was it Sarah put it?—like a big old watermelon, all over the floor.

Don't get sad, get mad—clever Mel. But even rage is overcome, overwhelmed—by what? Despair, maybe. A weight far heavier than sadness.

You look like a good woman, Adele said. Lila doesn't feel good. She puts her head back and closes her eyes.

"Lila," he says. "Lila, listen." Must she? "Please understand," she can imagine him crying as the plane plunges, all the way to the end. His last words to her: "Please understand."

He might want to be careful, here in this small, inescapable place.

Lila's quiet, large-handed father knotted ropes around a tree branch in the back yard and carved out a wooden swing seat for her and Don. She learned to pump and, entranced, began flying higher and higher, catching glimpses through the speeding air of greenery and fences, neighbouring gardens, and up, up until she faced leaves and sky at the moment of hovering, before the downward return. Then back, as far and high as she'd flown forward. She was tempted to try to finish the spiral, whirling right over, crashing through limbs and leaves. She never quite gained the momentum, but sometimes felt close.

Now she seems again to be flying high in one direction, hitting that moment of stillness at the top, then falling back, and up in the opposite direction, from one extreme to another.

She learned to get off the swing by letting it slow gradually; by digging hard into the ground with the soles of tough shoes; or by letting go and leaping dangerously free.

"Listen, Lila," he says again in that voice, and she braces herself. He will say first something like, "You know I love you." His pledges of affection, whether he has noticed or not, are too often a prelude to some unhappy announcement.

"You know I love you." And it's true, he does. Love isn't clear as glass, however. And surely he hasn't confused it with romance, a far more transparent matter.

Still, he must have a heart that's simply huge, to contain as much as it does. Imagine wishing for a man to have a smaller heart!

He may think her smile is for him. "The thing is, Lila, if you're right and this plane does go down" (did she say that? Not recently, she thinks, if ever. And it's hardly a matter of her opinion. If that counted, much would be different, and not just up here), "if it happens, it puts me in a terrible position."

No kidding. If dead is a terrible position, he'll be in one for sure. Along with her, and everyone else here.

"You know what I mean." She sighs. Yes, she does. "And you were gone for a long time, and you seemed so angry." Yes, yes, her fault, no doubt, with her messy, negative emotions. She hears herself snort.

It's true she can be disruptive and annoying at important moments; it's not that she doesn't feel for him.

His voice hardens. "I have to think about them, Lila, be fair! Think how it'll feel for Dorothy, not just finding out she's a widow, but all this, too, and the girls—what will they be left to imagine? And I have a grandson, you know. I don't want him growing up with the idea his grandfather was an asshole." He is very concerned about what people will think of him, it seems to Lila. He is as intent on his place in history as any ambitious politician.

"So I've been writing a letter to them." She knows that. "I realize it's almost impossible anybody would find it, or be able to read it if they did, but I needed to try."

"To what?"

She feels his shoulders rise and fall beside her. "To explain, I guess. To leave word of some kind. A message. I know it doesn't make sense, but it's stupid just sitting here, and I hate what they're going to think."

They have returned to his regret at dying with her.

Look at it this way: if he were sitting in a doomed plane beside his wife or either of his daughters, the chances are remote that he would open his briefcase, pull out paper and pen and start writing a last letter to Lila. Telling her just how this happened; knowing what she would think, how she would feel, needing to make clear his affections.

He would never be able to explain such an activity.

Opening her eyes, she finds him regarding her anxiously, little crinkles in his forehead. "So?" she asks. "What do you want me to say? Do what you need to do, I don't care."

Evidently he wants more than for her not to care. His mouth tightens the way it does when her reverence for his family fails, as it always naturally does, to match his. When she comes up short of his hopes.

His family is their most dangerous territory. Now they are on this most dangerous territory in a most dangerous circumstance. It seems there are different kinds of radiance. This one creates quick, bright sparkles of electricity between them.

There's enough fire outside, without starting interior conflagrations as well.

"You seem to have found a lot to say." There are pages of writing—is he planning to hurl his explaining, pleading eloquence into the sea in a very large bottle?

"No." He looks defeated. "There aren't any good words. Only, at least if it was ever found, they'd know I tried. But of course all of it's hopeless. I can't say what I mean, and nobody'll find it anyway."

"Have you finished?"

"Almost. A few more minutes? Look, Lila, I know it's a lot to ask, but for me? A few more minutes?"

What the hell. "Go ahead. Desperate times for you, apparently, so I'm sure you require desperate measures."

Her voice is dry as a desert, but he hears, it seems, what he wants to. "Thank you." He no longer looks even faintly angry. "I'm so grateful for you, Lila."

Yes, she'd have to imagine he's pretty lucky, all right. And he doesn't even know the extent of his good fortune. He appears to have no idea how close he has come to the perilous, unsturdy edge of tolerance, her capacity for absorbing blows and keeping more or less silent.

Or she could have brought Adele along to chew at him over holy promises.

Where's Adele gotten to? Looking around, Lila can't spot her, or Sarah for that matter. Jimmy and Mel, she sees, stretching to look back, are holding each other, limbs twined till they look like a single person. Or a single peony.

Some people pray, curse or cry, some stare into space. Lila supposes she herself is one of the space-starers. Behind those still faces, thoughts and pictures must simply be racing.

Tom looks to be one of the few actually doing something. It must be another habit that dies hard; or it might be accounted for by a historian's impulse to leave a record of events, and to summarize meanings. Shouldn't a lover of literature have a similar inclination, although more likely to leave a sonnet, or a meditation, a sharp thought on last moments? A mordant, Anne Sextonish taunt? Anne Sexton spent her whole life journeying towards death, though, before she simply stopped waiting and grabbed it. Ill prepared in comparison, Lila might only be able to come up with a bit of doggerel, catchy, brittle and bright.

Still, under the circumstances, even that much should impress whoever she addressed it to. And just who would that be?

Tom has spoken highly of the miracle of offspring. "They change your life in astonishing, entirely unpredictable ways." So it seems.

By now any children she'd had would be like Tom's, grown up and out of her hands, off in their own lives, like Jimmy and Mel. By today she could have had twenty-odd years with people she can't, at this point, begin to imagine.

What is he telling his loved ones, scribbling away on his pad of lined paper? Something like, "You changed my life in astonishing, entirely unpredictable ways"?

If he weren't here beside her, Lila might want to write Tom. But which words? Different ones under that circumstance than under this one. "I want you to know I adored you," she might have said, "and loved and enjoyed you." Or "You helped me to be better and stronger. Much stronger." She could say, "I've had astounding pleasure from your skin and bones." She might want to say, "Thank you."

She could do that now, for that matter; could pass scrawled notes to him, also throwing in, "You bastard," perhaps, for some abusive balance.

This must be why people weep and cry out. Words aren't enough. Even raw sounds aren't enough; there's nothing so loud or so fierce it can capture the volume of grief or pace of emotion in this space.

Does anyone at all look content? Is anyone thinking, "Hey, I did my best, it was a pretty good run, it's okay if it's over"? People always want more. Lila does, too.

She hasn't been a cruel or violent or particularly vicious person. She hasn't caused any grave disasters or told many huge lies, or injured puppies and kittens.

Equally, though, she has not committed many large or deliberate kindnesses, only the kind any remotely sane and humane person would perform. The time, say, leaving a drugstore, she found a child alone and frightened on the sidewalk, sobbing for "My daddy" and "My mummy." He was little and very damp and so scared he was choking on his own breath. Naturally Lila stopped—who wouldn't?

She knelt and hugged him, although she was a bit nervous about touching him. "It's okay, we'll take care of you, don't worry, everything will be fine." Holding his hand, she went back into the drugstore, called the police, bought the child a small chocolate bar to eat while they waited together outside.

First the police came, then finally a frantic parent pelted around the corner. "Oh my god, oh my god," the father said, "I don't know how to thank you. I was terrified, what might have happened." Lila couldn't help noticing he spoke first of his own terror, not his son's. He hugged the little boy, then shook him. "Don't you ever, ever do that again," he said in a voice menacing with the rage of relief. "My god, you're a mess. What're you doing with that chocolate?"

Lila's own small act contained no particular goodness, though. It was performed at least partly in her own interests, just as her mother carried out her far more numerous and habitual kindnesses. Lila's mother's good works kept her very busy. They also gave her the power not only of a great deal of sorrowful information, but also of having gained it through incontrovertibly virtuous methods. Lila's kindnesses have simply allowed her to sleep at night. She would never have been rid of pictures of harm to that little lost boy if she'd walked past him because, if she paused, she'd be late for a class.

Indeed, she missed a class. There were complaints.

Don't all kinds of apparent goodness consist partly of self-interest? Because one can't bear to picture the alternatives? Tom calls this view cynical, although she can't think how the word applies. They had rather a brisk discussion—argument—one night over how they each regard acts of seeming altruism.

And see, even now he may think she's concerned for his desires at the expense of her own, sitting here quietly, letting him write. Saint Lila of the Nurturers.

She could write Patsy and Nell, or Don or his children, but what would she say? Something like, "I'm really glad to have known you, and I hope you will think of me, too, with affection. I'm scared, but I guess I would have been scared at the end anyway. I'm also in an extremely bad mood at the moment, but it's nothing to do with you.

"I'd like to have been better, but you never know, do you? More or less, I've enjoyed myself, and by and large I've done what I wanted. I might have some bigger ideas now that I've had this day, but I guess it's too late, so what can I say except that I'm terribly frightened but not, as it turns out, vastly unhappy, if you see what I mean by the difference. If I'd known and felt before what I know and feel now, I might have done differently or better, but I didn't, so that's that. It was grand to know you, you added much to my time with you, and I hope your lives go well. You might want to consider last moments. They're actually quite interesting."

Even fashioned into iambic pentameter, these have no chance of becoming stirring greeting-card words.

Tom's pen is moving swiftly; he must have lots to say. Does he find himself baffled by the banality of his emotions when they're set down flat on paper?

Perhaps he is more eloquent than she, or wants to discuss specific events more than she would. She does hope he isn't writing a confessional; even by her standards that would be disgustingly selfish, self-conscious, self-absorbed.

"You okay?" he asks, glancing up briefly.

"Just fine." He has the nerve to reach over absently to touch her hand. "But what are you finding to say?"

It's private, of course. He looks vaguely towards her shoulder instead of her eyes. "Just things about what different people mean to me, I guess. Some things that are important to me. Like that I want my girls to know how much I love them."

Anyone else?

"But what, specifically?" She smiles at him in her brightest, most disinterested way, another lie, oh dear. And why bother? Except there may be no more chances. "Because you know, what you say to them is a message to me, too. Since I fit in the gaps between all those words and feelings, I'm curious about what those gaps are at the moment."

He gets angry when she says things like that. He should be careful.

How foolish, though, and sad. Like those men wrestling red-faced in the aisle.

"For god's sake, Lila. All this time and you can still say that—I don't know any more ways to say who you are to me. What you mean." He sighs. "If you don't know now, you never will, I guess."

Heaven knows that's true.

"I've been watching you," said the man who turned out to be Tom, more than five years ago.

She knew who he was, but women have to keep on their toes, judging possible menaces. Also campuses, like some small, very rural, very isolated communities, tend to breed their own varieties of weirdness.

He saw what she was thinking and laughed. She has always been alert to the shapes of men's hands and the quality of their laughter. His hands were still in his pockets, but his laughter rolled out with delight. "For no evil reason, honest." He has a winning, glinting smile. He is a man with charm. Perhaps, knowing she was a professor of literature, he mistook her for someone poetic, or soft.

Over their drink in the faculty lounge, he grinned. "You looked at me as if I might be a stalker, or a serial killer."

"Well yes. And you might be, mightn't you?" But she was smiling, too.

Weeks later, he said, "This is terrible. What should we do?" As if she were an emperor, he handed her power over the life or death of love: thumbs up, thumbs down.

Who turns thumbs down on love, except for saints and martyrs?

Later still, he told her, "You have no idea how much courage it took to go up to you. I thought, 'Maybe she'll say no. She's a smart woman, and that would be the smart thing to do.' But I also thought, 'Come on, Tom, you have to. If you don't, you'll wonder till your dying day.'"

How lightly such expressions trip off the tongue. Once, Lila had a blind student to whom she gave extra help. She was horrified by how often she heard herself saying, "So you see," or "Picture this."

"It's all right," he told her finally. "I do see, in my head, and anyway I know it's just an expression. Don't worry." He had the wandering, unfocused eyes some blind people have, and was a ferociously determined young man. What has happened to him, has his ferocious determination kept him speeding forward, whatever forward meant to him, whatever it was he was aiming for? As she recalls, he wanted to be a meteorologist, but that sounds peculiar and may not be right.

"Love is in the air"—another expression, or a song. As if it's contagious, a virus. Well, at the time Lila happened to be vulnerable, and it leaped to her skin, and came to infect her. And certainly it's been an interesting disease.

Only, like measles or chicken pox, not always an attractive one.

In the lounge she regarded Tom's fingers surrounding the Scotch glass and judged them to be competent and strong. A surgeon's hands, she might have imagined, if she hadn't already felt the hands of a surgeon. Even if she'd known it would come to this moment, she'd have to say she does not regret him. There was promise, and on the whole she would have to say it's been kept.

Only, he has multiple promises to keep. He is still a politician, juggling various interests, and his constituency is inordinately large.

"One more minute," he says. "Okay?" He must be running out of ways to explain himself.

Here is one of the questions that govern civility: what would be the result if everyone behaved as you do? If everyone behaved as Tom and Lila have, the world of love and promises would be an anarchy. They have made exceptions of themselves.

If everyone here unleashed full, true emotions, the result would also surely be anarchy. People would get badly hurt, some might be killed. And that would be without even crashing. It would look very foolish indeed if the plane landed safely, but with a cargo of dead and mutilated passengers who had turned on each other.

Although of course disaster does bring out the virtue in some. Just as, no doubt, some people do turn thumbs down on love.

It must be hard for him to find a way to end his letter. Will "Love, Tom" do the trick? Or "Sincerely"?

Goodbyes are by nature troublesome. They may be right, necessary or inevitable, but they are also sad and frightening.

Tom is tamping his pages into line on his lap—would he like to read them over, see what he's done? He leans to his briefcase, opens it, removes a large brown envelope, folds the sheets inside it. Who will it be addressed to? His wife only? His wife and two daughters?

"To my family," he scrawls, uneasily shifting the envelope so that it's difficult for her to see.

He tucks it all back in the briefcase, which Lila supposes makes as much sense as tucking it anywhere else.

Won't briefcases sink? Won't they hit the water like rocks, then spin slowly to the bottom of the ocean, far beyond even light? She imagines his briefcase settling into sediment and rock, being nudged by strange, curious sea creatures. All those pages will soak up salt water. Their ink will run, turn liquid; his words will become a tiny portion of foreign matter, an infinitesimal pollution in the sea-scheme of things.

"To my family." Well.

She has known and touched at one time or another every line and wrinkle of the face he now turns to her. She is familiar with each eyelash and every curling hair of eyebrows and with the whiskers which these days come in grey each afternoon. He has more lines at the sides of his eyes and his mouth than when they met. Today they look especially deep and permanent.

This is the day everything about them may finally become permanent. Hardly what she had in mind; like that old warning, "Be careful what you wish for."

When he looks at her so intently, does he recognize every eyelash and hair, every wrinkle and line, each mark and freckle? "My dear," he says, reaching to stroke her cheekbone with his finger. "Thank you." So she supposes he does.

"Remember," he asks, "the accident?"

Oh yes, their only previous encounter with disaster.

Strange, really, how little experience a woman her age may have with life-threatening crisis, a different matter from loss or grief or heartache. What an amateur she is in some regards.

People must skirt death all the time, something slipping near and sliding away again, sometimes unnoticed, sometimes glimpsed. "Whew!" they say if they do spot the moment. "That was close." And on they go.

"I was thinking how brave you were, and sturdy." He smiles. "You didn't even complain about losing the car. You're an awfully good companion in an emergency."

Less appealing, it seems, as a day-to-day companion, not to mention one to die with. "Thank you," she says.

That accident he speaks of, a couple of years ago, was if nothing else a dramatic example of the perils of simply sitting beside each other, trying to do something together. They failed, it appears, to take it sufficiently to heart—how easily people forget lessons, warnings, little parables of misfortune.

But what are the odds?

That accident was quite different from this, however. It required much frantic action, instead of this frantic in-action, and it also took only a moment, nothing like this business of life or death hanging suspended; although it was a long moment: an instant when suddenly a car was coming straight at them over the hill ahead, passing when it shouldn't, but no one was sorting out rights and wrongs just then.

It had a slow-motion quality, as accidents do, each movement bright and distinct, as if there were all the time in the world. She remembers Tom's desperate turns of the wheel, the nasty, helpless sliding, sunlight reflecting off brown fenders and silver ones, the rich greens of roadside grasses. She remembers thinking, Oh my god, and then, Now we're caught, which later she found interesting. Also later she was able to consider questions of chance: that if Tom hadn't been the one driving, they might have been killed. If Tom hadn't freed a weekend to spend with her, neither of them would have been on that road in the first place, headed towards a beach and an overpriced, out-of-the-way inn.

But alert, quick-reflexed Tom was driving, although it was her car, which also turned out to be a blessing of sorts. He swore and braked and swerved and twisted, and they flew and rocked and screeched until they were, yes, halted and right side up in a ditch of glorious wild tiger lilies, the car's front end crushed into the bank of the ditch so hard the dash at her knees would have collapsed in the next moment. As it was, the radio was twisted and her tapes were wrecked.

There must have been sounds around them, but Lila recalls absolute stillness. They reached for each other's hands and sat staring ahead, absorbing the abrupt change of situation and view. Finally they became aware of excited voices and worried faces around them. Other vehicles were pulling up, stopping. She and Tom looked at each other at last. "You okay?" he asked, and she nodded.

"You?" and he nodded.

They pushed at crumpled, protesting doors and got out.

People hovered, offered help, blankets, places to sit, somebody had gone off to call ambulances, police. They asked anxious questions, tried to get her and Tom to lie down or to be embraced. It felt like waking up in winter, feeling cold air with fingertips and nose, but cosy under the comforter. How kind people were, Lila thought.

"We'll be fine," she assured them. "We're lucky, it's only the car that got hurt." She put a hand on Tom's shaken shoulder. "Thank heavens you're such a good driver. You saved our lives, you know." He straightened, and even smiled a little.

"Your car," he said. "I'm sorry."

"It doesn't matter."

By the time the police arrived, they were reasonably steady and able to tell what had happened, as did several witnesses, and it was a very good thing that none of it was Tom's fault, and an exceptionally good thing the kids in the other car weren't much hurt, so that Tom and Lila could escape the next step of public scrutiny. If the event had been serious or fatal, there would have been a story in a newspaper. Even a paragraph in print would have ruined them.

After ambulances had taken everyone involved to the nearest hospital in the nearest little town, and they'd been checked and treated for, mainly, mild shock, they looked for ways to tell each other how relieved they were and how lucky they'd been. Not wanting, though, to say aloud specifically and precisely which disasters they'd dodged, besides death, they didn't get much beyond "We're so lucky." Anyway, they both knew. Words were more than unnecessary, they risked a perilous opening of wounds when they were already slightly wounded.

Lila's car was towed and Tom went off to rent one to get them home. It was hours before, having given up on the getaway, they were back at Lila's house, unlocking Lila's door, collapsing on Lila's sofa, safe and invisible again behind Lila's walls.

They were tentative, however, for one reason and another, about touching. It seemed the sort of event that drew them intensely together, but also hurled them apart in the sharp reminder of drastically different, unbridgeable circumstances.

But they've made many small trips in which nothing worse happened than returning home.

If this plane goes down, it'll amount to a lot more than a paragraph. She imagines police and reporters knocking on doors, making announcements, seeking pictures and reactions and epitaphs.

"And remember," he asks, "the snowstorm we drove through that other weekend?"

Yes again. Another tribute to his driving skills, a long, white-knuckled, headachy journey. But what is he playing at, with this do-you-remember? Is it what he played at in his letter? An appeal to past, in hopes it will overwhelm present?

"I felt perfectly safe," she says, "but bad for you." Arriving at last in their hotel room, they'd thrown off their clothes in celebration. "You were exhausted."

"Not *too* exhausted, I hope."

"Not right away." It is, after all, a happy memory. "But you were snoring by the time room service came. I had to throw the bedspread over you and hustle into my robe. Hotel people must wonder what they're getting into every time they knock on a door."

"The place tonight doesn't have room service, so we won't have to worry about that." Probably that's intended to reassure that, once again, their future will triumph. Kind words, and brave ones, no doubt; although sabotaged by his letter.

"I remember calling you late at night because I wanted to hear your voice, even if it wasn't fair, waking you up." She'd imagined him slipping out of bed and downstairs to some private room, cautiously punching her number, keeping his voice low. She was pleased by his efforts, the care he took; although would have preferred, naturally, to be wakened by a voice and a body beside her.

It's a long time since he's made one of those calls. They both must have learned to sleep soundly.

"I never minded. I loved hearing your voice. I'd wake up in the morning thinking about talking to you. Sometimes I kept remembering right into class, and I'd have to pace to give my body something to do."

"When I had thoughts like that, I had to sit very still behind my desk, so nobody could see what was on my mind."

They have gone deep into the past tense.

"I was thinking, I could have had a heart attack when I was forty, forty-two, like a lot of guys, and I would have missed you entirely. I'm glad we've had this much." There are no ceremonies for people like them; any pledges that get made are folded inside other kinds of words. But they are precious, and they do cause seams and cracks in the heart.

"Although," he adds, smiling slightly, "I could do with a lot more."

"Me too."

"Remember the beach?"

"I remember trying to get you to make love underwater, but you wouldn't."

"I think I didn't know how, exactly, but I was too proud to admit it. I'm sorry I made us miss it. Remember the time I went along to the reception your department was giving for that poet, what's his name? Somebody famous I'd never heard of."

"Who got so pissed, and threw up. And then we sneaked out. You gave me a wink and left, and I waited a few minutes and followed. It was like being fifteen again, necking in your car."

"The hormones were pretty adolescent too."

"I thought it was grand to be steaming up car windows at forty-two. If also reckless."

"Even grander and more reckless for me, at forty-four."

"We were lucky."

"I've always felt lucky, knowing you."

That's nice. Did he write something similar to the people of his family, but with a slightly varied spin to make it personal to them?

Oh, it doesn't matter, doesn't matter. Except it does.

Wouldn't he be a hero, though, if his letter were found. People would say not only, "Look how he cared right to the end, look at those words of devotion and hope." Which she assumes they are, or are intended to be. They would also say, "Imagine a man of such calm, such fortitude and generosity, spending his very last moments thinking of others, and ways to comfort."

His words would be printed in newspapers and portrayed on television screens, a testament to his cool head, warm heart.

People would measure themselves by Tom and his words. They would wonder, "Could I have done such a thing?" or "What would I have written, if it were me? Who would I write to, and what would I most want to tell them?"

The survivors of other passengers might feel somewhat ashamed of their loved ones, for their absence of eloquence at the end. Or they might feel reassured that perhaps Tom spoke for them all, and that their loved ones also died well.

Around the globe, people would be stirred and astonished by Tom and his effort and words.

A far smaller circle would also be asking, "What do you suppose he and Lila were doing together? It surely wasn't coincidence." Or "Boy, that's a whole heap of bad luck, isn't it? Way to get caught in front of the world." Or "What nerve, writing something like that."

Tom has no doubt also considered all this. It certainly doesn't bear mentioning.

"You know," Lila says, "I bet all sorts of things happen to planes that we never hear about. Maybe this isn't even so unusual, and the crew knows exactly what they're doing."

"Yeah, well, check out the flight attendants—do they look as if they're taking this for granted, or even know what they're doing?"

Not really. Three of them, including Sheila, are together, whispering. Sheila's hands are in motion, making gestures Lila can't interpret, another is frowning, and the third looks merely harassed. It's possible they're worried about running low on coffee and soft drinks, but it looks as if what they've run out of is gloss. Things like lipstick and wisps of hair have come unstuck. Their glitter has worn off and what remains is unshiny, unauthoritative. Earthbound and ordinary.

In a situation requiring them to be more than human, to look merely human is—what's the word Lila wants?— yes, disquieting. At best, disquieting, an unruffled, minor word, not too upsetting as words go in potential disasters.

Disaster is a good one to avoid. Cataclysm. Catastrophe. Tragedy.

But that's a word, like fate, with nice, compact literary meaning, having to do with Oedipus, Lear, people like that, not people like Tom or herself, or Sarah, or Adele, or Jimmy or Mel, or Susie or her mother, or anyone else here, surely. Unhappy ends brought about by huge fatal flaws.

What would hers be? Or Tom's? Self-indulgence, she supposes. A reluctance to resist pleasing impulses. That seems very small.

"I can't find," she says, "a way to think about this. I find a lot of little ways, but not a proper big one. You're a historian, you're supposed to have perspective; do you get a better view?"

"Ah, Lila." He sighs. "You expect a good deal from history, don't you? Although you're right; if I look at this through the lens of centuries, there is a sort of universal pattern."

"Which is?"

He regards her solemnly.

"Shit happens."

That's why she's loved him. For a moment she stares, and then they're laughing, real heads-back, body-rocking, stomach-clutching, breath-taking laughter.

What a perfect moment for the plane to go down. Then they could just die laughing.

Weeping, screaming, throwing up—all that is apparently normal, but hoots of delight are unseemly and possibly disgraceful, and they've drawn some frowning attention.

"Oh dear," she says finally, "my stomach hurts."

"It would have been a good moment to go down, that's for sure."

She is startled, as she sometimes is, when he speaks her thoughts. But after more than five years, it's hardly eerie if they know more about each other than they're aware of knowing.

"Anyway," he says, "I think I understand better why you were laughing before. I'm sorry."

Apology or regret? That question again; but perhaps, like some others, no longer very important.

nine

SHEILA MOVES ALONG
the aisle, speaking up to be heard. "If those of you nearest
the windows will draw down your blinds, we'll be starting the movie. I apologize for the delay." She smiles,
rather shakily, Lila thinks. "I understand it's an excellent
film, and we also apologize in advance because we should
be on the ground long before it ends."

Lila herself couldn't have made a worse joke.

"I mean," Sheila goes on quickly, "we'll be happily
landed at Heathrow."

Then why start it? What is it passengers shouldn't see
that requires the shades to be pulled? The plane tugs
slightly right, slightly left. A man Lila can barely make out,
sitting in an aisle seat a few rows ahead, grabs Sheila's arm.

"What the fuck's going on?" His voice is loud and
harsh, and around him people stir anxiously. "Don't give

us that shit about movies, we want to know what's really happening."

Do they?

"Please, sir, just stay in your seat. Everything's fine, there's no cause for concern. Those small movements are just manoeuvres. The pilot and co-pilot are doing exactly what they've been advised to do."

Does she know that? Does she believe it?

"Bullshit. And I wasn't leaving my fucking seat, so don't tell me to stay in it. We're in this crate, we deserve some decent information, and I want an answer to my fucking question." The man does seem to be capturing a mood; angry voices sound around him in grumbling support.

Sheila's eyes and lips narrow briefly, as if she would very much like to slap him. Then she looks as if she could cry, but mustn't do that, either. She looks, actually, like a kid with a part in a school play that's gone off the rails, out of control, into some spiralling, impromptu ad lib. Even her make-up looks stagey and garish against skin gone white.

"Sir, you're causing a disturbance, upsetting other passengers." She takes a deep breath, glances around. Gauging support or hostility? "Even if you're afraid, it's no reason to try to scare others. Particularly when there's nothing to be frightened of."

Oh, inspired, Lila thinks. The man is left voiceless, bruised where it hurts worst, in his pride. Others briefly roused by his fury now try to look as if they never were.

On the other hand. On the other hand, if Lila were the one demanding better information, she would not care to be treated with contempt. She would hope to phrase her concerns more politely, with more compassion for Sheila and for her fellow passengers, but equally she would hope not to hear drivel like, "There's nothing to be frightened of." She narrows her eyes as Sheila advances more confidently, pursuing the lowering of blinds. Which, astonishingly, do obediently descend.

Are these people crazy? How can they agree to shut themselves in, blocking out brightness for what may be their last moments? Shouldn't they need to bathe in light, feel awed and grateful that there still is such a thing as light?

Perhaps they're exhausted from seeing. From fear. The entire space is dimming, and Lila is having trouble catching her breath. Tom nudges her. "The blind? Can you reach it?"

Is he crazy, too? "Tom, it's too—eerie." That's the only word she can think of that isn't quite panicky. "Surely you don't want to watch the movie, do you?"

"I don't suppose so." He looks dubious, though; tempted. "But other people might. Especially the kids, it'll divert them." He nods towards Susie, but her eyes are closed, so she's not a good example. "And you know it won't be dark. There's always light."

Not the right kind, there won't be. Not real, true light.

How long would it take, starting now, for the plane to spin down to the sea? And what would the view be? What shifting, changing forms might light take during the descent?

"The blind please, ma'am." Sheila is beside Tom, looking at her, but Lila can't move, any more than she would be able to move a razor against her own wrist. Sheila reaches behind and pulls it down herself. "Thank you," says Tom. And "Sorry."

Lila's hands curl into fists, fingernails digging into the flesh of her palms. She closes her eyes, tries to conjure up light, and almost succeeds.

She hears Tom sigh, feels him fiddling with his headset.

In her mind's eye, she must be able to hold all the

shades of brightness: the blue and gold and green of sky, sunshine, grass, all that. The bright, comforting red is velvet, best dress from childhood, worn on special occasions, such as birthday parties. She can feel it too, under fingers, brushing thighs, a lost sensation.

Here's the lawn, a pricklier softness, that her father cultivated to a very particular colour and height, reluctantly and regularly mowed by Don. How rigorously their father judged and cared for that lawn, its uniform colour, its absence of weeds—he was meticulous about it, pacing it in the evenings, bending to run a palm over it, plucking offending presences from it. His extensive concern for something so inessential made him seem foolish.

What could that passion have really been for? Surely not truly for the perfection of grass.

Lila has made assumptions about her father and her mother, not all of which are necessarily borne out in these details. She has bestowed the word "seething" on her mother, and allowed her various passions, but has left her father sitting, quiet and kind, in a corner.

That's not where he was. He was out scrutinizing his lawn, or driving Don to hockey practice, or building the swing, or hammering and sawing away in the basement. Passing Lila, he might hug her shoulders, wordlessly. In his work, handing out and denying bank loans and mortgages, he must have been powerful.

He obviously had a part in whatever caused her mother to seethe; and her mother may have had a part in his solitary silences.

Lila's mother gave her, in a little blue cardboard box, her first pair of earrings: silver drops. Her father said, "Looks like you're getting all grown up." He sounded sad, and if Lila hadn't been fifteen and aimed towards her own deeply desired, undefined future, she might have spared him a moment of pity. If she tilted her head in a certain way, under the white-globed front hallway light, the earrings' silveriness glowed back at her from the long mirror by the door.

What was different then, wearing those earrings? Blind, dumb, ruthless hope, she supposes. Being young.

Now there are some questions she wouldn't mind asking her parents. But she missed any moment there might have been, and there is no point, and no time, to regret. She needs to keep her eye on the light.

Setting off on a cross-country road trip with her first lover, she drove through miles and miles of golden grain, light rippling over it, stirred by the wind. She can see the shiftings and colours more clearly than the lover, Jason, whose affections did not survive the rigours of their days together in the car, who grew hunched and morose, who was not much of a lover anyway, and who is unattached in her mind's eye to light.

After the prairies they wound through mountains, where brilliance glared off snow at the peaks, and lit lower rocks, and finally faded into hazy darkness below.

At the end of that journey, Lila was diverted from farewells, hers and Jason's, by sunlight like shatterings of glass skipping over the sea, far into the distance. She was awed by this first view in her life of the sea, couldn't imagine its depth and immensity.

Don't think of oceans.

All right then, cosy events. Fireside embraces, seductive, soft words.

Don't think of flames. Lila's eyes fly open.

On the screen, someone is riding a horse down a mountain. It looks like a dimmed, dulled version of her bright younger vision.

Some people actually appear to be staring at the screen, watching this. Surely, though, what they see are not horses and men, but scenes and films from their own lives.

What gorgeous duster coats the men in the movie are wearing. Look how they hang, how they move with those lanky bodies, how seductively they flare at the hips. She should get one—would she look properly dramatic, or just ridiculous?

Oh, how stupid—she won't be shopping for a duster coat, or anything else; another of those foolish, startled griefs.

Glancing at Tom, she is astonished to see that while he is watching the screen, headset clamped around his dishevelled, greying and receding hair, tears are simply flowing from his eyes, pouring unchecked down his face and off his chin. She has never seen him weep before. He is doing it without sound or movement, and it looks remarkable.

It's also private; as intrusive, and even embarrassing, to watch as it would be to walk into a room expecting to find it empty, and discovering instead a friend making love, catching in the eyes that remote and ardent look of orgasm.

One would back out, awkward and apologizing if seen, silent if not.

When Lila cries, which isn't often, her face contorts, her nose reddens, her hands fly up to catch and blot the tears. How can he weep without moving?

And what is he weeping for? Perhaps his own private version of prairies, or silver drop earrings.

She is struck to the heart that she has no idea, actually feels her heart quiver and lurch. Tears come to her own eyes. He has been the dearest person in her life, and at the end, she doesn't know what pictures form the contents of his grief, and he has no way of knowing hers. This sorrow is explosive; she could burst open, splashing loneliness over everything.

Well. Almost everyone must be deep inside their own soul when they die.

She closes her eyes, this time to be clear about what really may happen: smoke and spinning and blackness and burning light, limbs and voices flying and crying—all this can happen at any instant, and they would each be alone. It's going to hurt so much. Her poor skin, poor bones, all crumpled and crushed, and her beloved little home, and Don and Anne and the kids, the remnants of family, and all her beautiful books and ideas and words, and rows of young faces watching her, more or less eagerly, taking apart all those books and ideas with the hope and intention of being able to put them back together, and voices and laughter of gossiping colleagues and dear Patsy and Nell, in cafeterias and restaurants, in kitchens and living rooms and in voices on telephones. And mysterious, unknown Tom. Skin, voice, flesh over bones, fingers and palms on her flesh and his. Laughter and opposing ideas and desires, magical intersectings of ideas and desires, and solemn eyes, delicious lips. Her own secrets and dreams: whatever they are, her true final companions.

Opening her eyes, she finds Tom regarding her, now dry-eyed and dry-cheeked, with yet another queer and unfamiliar expression. "What?" she asks. In the end, it's not only words that have no life-saving uses. Love doesn't, either.

The end may be a matter of passionate, grieving silence when all else fails.

The cabin seems to sway and shift. She can't tell if it's the plane or herself.

Now he is stroking that thinnest layer of skin on the back of her hand; his thumb moving gently between her wrist and her fingers, and his fingers resting in her palm, connect her to her own skin, in this seat, in this cabin, in this instant.

Something will happen very soon, for very good or very ill. "It'll be all right," he says. "We'll be fine."

As if he knows. As if it's up to him. In their other lives, he knew and it was up to him, but there's no room here for the tininess of that plot, those small bumpings and grindings of emotion and event. She smiles at him anyway.

"I know we've had troubles," he says, "but I've never not loved you. You made my life more than I could have hoped."

She notices, although he may not, the past tense. "Thank you. You, too." Because it's perfectly true, he has made her life larger, no lie. There are pictures and ideas and touches and combinations of words she might never in her life have encountered, if he hadn't invited her for a drink.

The plane judders and something that feels large and vital grinds. Lila's skin is suddenly boiling, and Tom also breaks out in a sweat: exactly that, beads and drops popping out on his forehead, his neck, his hands.

The juddering slows, the grinding eases. This isn't it, then, not quite yet?

The cabin is oddly, briefly quiet. People must be shocked into silence, petrified into immobility. Everyone must be staring at something inside their own heads, behind their own eyes, beyond denial.

If all these people do vanish at once from their own lives, many stories will be changed. For generations, for the rest of life on earth for that matter, connections will be altered or lost, some unanticipated children will be born from unexpected unions, and some others will not. Some people may fall into poverty, and others will thrive. The hearts of thousands will be affected, and even some aspects of Tom's long view, history itself, will be altered. Lost lives, lost genes, lost prospects and possibilities—all that. A peace accord signed here, an unnecessary battle erupting there. Perhaps also a serial killer or two fewer in the future as well, who knows? Or one or two more.

Another shudder, another jolt, a fragile levelling.

When Lila was little, she performed a small daily ritual. First thing each morning, she said, just to herself, "Let something good happen. Let the first thing that happens be lucky." A small lucky event could expand to a whole lucky day; and the reverse.

It wasn't, she supposes, more ridiculous than other rituals of hope. Even heading for this flight, she was considering small events in a similar light, little moments of good fortune signifying much larger, far-flung fortunes. And look how that is turning out.

When she was little, she hunted four-leaf clovers, extremely rare and lucky to find in her father's immaculate lawn. She had no idea then what real good luck was, or real bad luck.

Real bad luck would have been to enter the world in a more brutal, unjust time or place. To unkind parents, or in a bleak location lacking shelter or food, or to a culture which required her feet to be bound, or her body mutilated, or one in which she would cook but never read, and certainly never teach the beauty of words, or anything else. What good luck, to have been able to eat, say, wear, do, possess, think, and love, more or less, within reason, what she desired. There can't be much more to ask of fortune; although she would now extend her hopes to not dying this way.

"My god," Tom says, "this is torture."

The level of movement and noise is rising again. Like him, people are regaining their voices, and what comes out once again is fear. Or maybe not, maybe she's wrong and it's regret, or despair. It's vigorous, at any rate, and feels volatile. "Sit down," Sheila commands, patrolling the aisle. "Take your seats. Nothing is happening, so just take your seats." She is no longer, Lila notes, saying "please," and is even touching some people rather roughly to force them back, or down.

How can they believe someone who says nothing is happening? How are they supposed to have faith in someone who has to push for obedience?

Whatever will happen, it's taking too long. Tom's right, it's excruciating, waiting and counting the notches carved into her life. "I wish," she says, trying to sound jaunty and brave, "we'd had our two weeks. If we were on our way back, I might not have minded so much." In fact, she might have been seeing other pictures entirely.

He fails to look charmed. "Can you feel that?" he asks urgently, clutching her hand.

Putting words into the air is not always wise. Unformed, unprepared ideas too easily vanish in speech; or the reverse: spoken aloud, they become too real, and unavoidable. Tom's anxiety, spoken aloud, makes Lila shiver.

What if she fell apart, broke into fragments of fear—how willing would he be to comfort and try to put her back together?

A terrible question to ask at this stage.

Everything is slippery and unfinished. Nothing she thought she had a grip on is firm. That should be appalling.

It almost feels hopeful.

Everyone, even those still flailing in their seats, or weeping, must be learning so much so fast—what a better teacher Lila would have been, if she could have stimulated this kind of desperate urgency in the classroom. "Learn or die," she could have commanded. "Understand, or you won't get out of this room alive." That would have sharpened them up, all right.

Oops. "Lila!" The plane lurches again to the right, cries and screams rise higher and Tom whispers, "Sweet

Jesus." Lila didn't know he had this streak of fundamen-
talism—next he'll be speaking in tongues.

But she, too, is again saying prayer-like words to herself: "Oh no, please no." If civility is thin, so, apparently,
is much else.

"Ladies and gentlemen," they hear. This time there's no
warning of the voice. The movie continues its westward
way on the screen, but abruptly without sound. "Ladies
and gentlemen this is your co-pilot, Frank McLean, again.
We regret if any of you have been alarmed by our most recent manoeuvres." The awful grinding hardly sounded
like a manoeuvre to Lila; it sounded more like metal on
the very edge of falling apart.

Christ, she's boiling in this sweater—to think she wore
it so her skin would be able to breathe. She plucks at it, to
unstick it from her skin. Tom has a little dip at the base of
his throat where sweat is starting to pool. What a *moist*
man he has been at times today.

"We want you to know that we remain on our course
and are making good progress. Within the next few minutes, we expect to reach the coast of England and be very
near our destination."

"Nearer My God To Thee"—that's what they sang on
the *Titanic*, isn't it? Or is that only a fable of courage?

"In order to maximize our position, we are advising
you of an action we have undertaken which will cause
some inconvenience when we arrive. To lighten the aircraft and facilitate our landing, we are releasing cargo
while we are still over water. We have almost completed
this process. When we arrive, therefore, passengers will
find themselves—yourselves—without luggage. Obviously we regret the loss of any items of value, and the inconvenience. However, the airline accepts responsibility,
and claim forms and some emergency supplies will be
available for you at our destination."

Oh, isn't that heartening—they'll know they're safe when they start filling out forms.

Lila wonders what she would miss, which items sea creatures would enjoy, or be puzzled by, as they hurtle into that dark world. Lace and cotton, even one new dress of extravagant silk—she packed, she remembers, with an eye to the creation of appealing memories.

Let the sea have them; if only it doesn't get her skin and bones.

She is astounded to hear some grumbling, people cranky about their possessions counting and mourning their losses. "I am sure," the voice goes on smoothly, "that you will all consider this a small sacrifice in comparison to the increased safety it provides."

On the movie screen, two men face each other down: a long, dark look exchanged. One of them, presumably, will shortly die. The film plays like white sound, a frivolous alternative vision.

"As to your carry-on luggage, you will not be able to exit the plane with it, but airport crews will retrieve it for you as soon as possible after we've landed."

Lila supposes he has to speak as if these things will actually occur.

Who knows, perhaps they will.

Tom will have to leave behind not only the bag stored beside hers overhead, but his precious briefcase with his precious letter. Still, if they were to land safely, he wouldn't need it, would he? He wouldn't even want it, explosive, haunting evidence.

People stick all kinds of things into carry-on luggage, now waiting above to roam bullet-like around the cabin. Random injury or death may come from inside, just as well as outside. At least this isn't a hijacking; although if it were, there'd be a dramatic focus instead of this terrifying empty waiting. People could try talking to a hijacker,

however unbalanced and unpredictable. There's no argu-
ing with metal, or fire, or air, or, for that matter, fate.

"Again, we regret the loss of your belongings, but we
are otherwise doing well and have every confidence in a
safe arrival. You can expect to be not only on the ground,
but sorted out and relaxing, in well under an hour." That
brings hopeful gasps—so soon! As if safety is merely a
matter of time.

"We are continuing our descent to lower altitudes and
again require you to remain sitting with your seatbelts
fastened. The aircraft is experiencing some decreased stability due to wing damage, as well as fluctuations in air
pressure. We are doing everything possible to compensate, but there may be occasional discomfort as a result,
and we ask you not to be alarmed."

The voice brightens. "And by the way, ladies and gentlemen, we are just now reaching the coastline and from
here on will be flying over southern England. For your
information, we're advised there are mild temperatures
and a light rain awaiting us on our arrival. See you at
Heathrow!"

And on that cheery note, the sound system clicks off.

How has the high-pitched pilot been occupying himself while the co-pilot speaks? Do his fingers fly from button to button and lever to lever as he dodges disaster? Did
he grin or grimace at the sight, at last, of coastline? He
must be concerned about the landing, if they get that far.
Lila knows she is.

She now sees him less as a scrawny man than a wiry
one. The mellifluous Frank McLean she imagines as
broad-shouldered, broad-chested, slim-hipped, long-
legged, blandly handsome. Those two men, along with
whoever else may form a cockpit crew on a plane like
this—are there others, or only computers?—must, like
Sheila and the other flight attendants, have been looking

forward to something at the end of the day. Lila hopes it's
something wonderfully compelling.

"Looks good," Tom says. "Don't you think?"

Well, just how does it look? Impulsively, Lila half
stands, reaches across the window seat to the shade, lifts
it slightly, peers out. "Jesus, Tom."

The world out there is almost entirely, beautifully, gloriously dark. The remaining tracings of light are from
faded sun, faint clouds. Not fire. The wing is somewhat
charred and cracked and curled, but "My god," she says,
turning towards him, "it's out."

He regards her with wild hope. She can smell his
slightly acrid sweat, and it seems to her the scent of being
alive.

Neither of them speaks further, and blinds are still
down, the movie still running, but once again news
spreads mysteriously. Around the grey cabin, faces light up
and voices brighten. A few shades are lifted on this side of
the plane, and on the other side a group of people move
into the aisle and dance in a cramped circle, holding hands
and whooping. Sheila, on this side, frowns at that side.

Again the whole space overflows with too much raw
emotion. Fear and hope jostle, poking out in bursts of
wild raucous laughter and sobs. Imagine living! Lila is
dazzled. She feels like an angel—a benevolent, weight-
less, silver-winged creature floating above all previous
understanding.

Surely they are each bound to feel, from now on,
every second of being alive. They'll be like old fabulous
paintings, crusted with grime, restored to their glowing,
mysteriously intended, original brightness. What a surprise, what a shock!

She stretches and arches, and even her scalp feels
alive, even the soles of her feet. "I think," Tom says, "I'm
going to have a heart attack from the relief."

"Please," Sheila is calling, "keep your seats." As if, Lila thinks, their collective helium joy could lift and tilt the plane off its frail course.

There is some slight weight, though, in the air and in Sheila's voice. Lila tilts her head to listen for something rumbling beneath the tears and jubilation.

What a lovely word, jubilation: all bells and laughter.

"Maybe," Tom glances at his watch, "in a couple of hours we'll be in the hotel bar drinking champagne. Or in bed drinking champagne. Celebrating being alive. Making a toast to going on, same as ever. Do you think?"

What she hears coming out of her mouth is, "I hope not."

Another surprise.

No time to think what she meant, Christ, the plane is dipping, its joints seem to shudder, it veers to the right, and down. "Jesus!" Tom cries, and Lila cries at the same instant, "No!" and they reach for each other. In Tom's eyes, Lila sees a renewal of terror; he must see the same in hers. There are dreadful sounds all around them.

They are going to die now, together, in grim, fleshy, bone-crushing catastrophe—Sarah, Adele, Jimmy the Web and Mel, Susie and her mother, the big guy by the emergency exit, Tom, herself—all locked spinning in an awful, intimate orgy of death. How fragile skin is, after holding everything together for so long.

Lila's eyes fly upward to where oxygen masks are waiting, but not descending. Perhaps they're useless anyway, or would only prolong the torment. In all the flights she has taken, she has never actually handled an oxygen mask. Nor has she been in a dark cabin with only those lines on the aisles to follow to safety—how does she know if they actually show up, or if they would be discernible beneath stampeding feet? And even if it's possible to get to an emergency exit, shove past the big man, push open the door, what then? A step into cold, diminishing space.

The plane is slipping, dropping, tipping, sliding sideways, like a car hitting ice. Lila faces head on into nothing—what a strange, breath-holding day, now a pinpoint of a moment.

She isn't afraid, exactly. She does feel in whole, intimate sympathy with this machine, this apparatus, this great, struggling metal being. Any shift of vibration under her feet, any alteration of pitch to her ears—it's like listening during those three terrible days to little Sam's heartbeats, taking any tiny movement or change as a sign of life, or of death. She feels the plane straining, the striving beat of its remaining engines, the tenderness of its skin. Like herself, it is a container for everything essential and perishable.

She urges it on with a kind of love for its brave, stubborn effort: go, go, you can do it. She wants to rock in her seat in encouragement, but also doesn't want to make it take into account any small, unbalancing movement.

It levels out, steadies, takes a deep breath. So does she. She pats an armrest, taps a foot: good plane, nice going, keep trying, you'll make it, hang in there.

Other people are swearing, praying, battling as if the plane is their enemy. Rebelling against the nature of the beast. Never mind, she tells it. Keep your eye on desire.

Tom turns awkwardly, generously, towards her; puts a hand on her face, the other on her arm, constrained by his seatbelt. "Almost there. Nearly safe." His long fingers are light on her cheek, and the faint brown hairs on the back of his other hand are light also. He is very kind, especially considering his fears at the end of even ordinary flights.

She has been delighted by his hands, and intimately fond of the dustings, wherever they occur on him, of fine hairs. He has strong bones, especially sturdy at the wrists.

There have been times she has dug her fingers into his flesh to find his skeleton, feel his structure, determine its soundness.

How arduously he has laboured on occasion to have everything. Everyone.

Do the words "arduous" and "ardour" have a common root?

Pay attention to the plane, suffering and determined, shuddering and trembling, trying so hard. It needs every strength she can give, and she has a great deal, it turns out: no end of passions, desires and hopes. Her enormous, thwarted will, and enormous, thwarted love.

It takes another dip and a swerve, but feels as if it has a better grip on itself. Tom's arm tightens. "Lila, I love you. Okay? If something happens, I love you." And if it does not?

"I know," she tells him.

These downward lurches must be bringing them closer and closer to the ground. After all, the ocean may have been a softer, more forgiving destination. People below, are they looking up, wondering? Are their attentions caught by a roaring much too near? Does the grinding make their teeth ache? How about the moans and screams, do they carry in the air, to the earth?

Or it's dark, and raining a bit, and most people have gone indoors for the evening. They're relaxing around fireplaces, television sets, kitchen tables. They've turned up lights, and children are laughing and squabbling, grown-ups are cooking or washing up and chatting over their various days, or quarrelling or gossiping or falling silent. Do they feel a sudden chill? A darkness? An unfamiliar kind of quiet? A shiver they can't put their fingers on?

It's hard to imagine that the rampaging emotions up here aren't leaking out, causing their own kind of lightning and an ominous thundering in the hearts of people passed over.

It would be gone quickly. Then, Lila imagines lights briefly looking brighter, and voices sounding clearer; figures more sharply perceived and more acutely considered. There is a brief, unaccountable moment in which people can see. An arm goes around a shoulder; a child is lifted into the air and embraced; people smile, expressions soften, eyes grow kind.

Or with a sudden pure vision a knife finally enters a belly that is no longer bearable.

"Lila," Tom says. His eyes look clear of feeling. She touches his hand but with her free hand strokes the armrest: dear plane, brave plane, stay up, do well. It rears and shudders, throwing Tom into her shoulder. "We must be close."

"I think so."

There ought to be so much to say.

"Ladies and gentlemen." The deep voice returns, and on the screen the movie skids to a ragged, quivering halt.

"We are now approaching Heathrow." There are scattered cheers, but also a further urgent tightening of belly muscles, shoulders, calves, biceps, backs. "Since this is being considered an emergency landing, we have been given priority and assistance. As you know, among our concerns is the damaged wing, which creates a number of difficulties, some of them quite minor." Some of them evidently major, as well, and by and large undefined.

"As a precaution, we are asking you to assume emergency landing position, which your flight attendants will demonstrate again and help you with. It's important everyone follow all instructions quickly and without discussion.

"When we're on the ground and have come to a halt, you will leave in orderly fashion through the emergency exits, which open automatically into slides to the tarmac. It is essential to proceed calmly." The big man by the nearest exit is sitting very straight and listening hard.

It's difficult to believe this is happening. Lila shakes her head, but it will not clear.

"Under no circumstances from this point may you leave your seat or undo your seatbelts. Parents must ensure their children are securely fastened and that they also follow all emergency instructions. We regret this has been a difficult flight, and wish to thank you all for your continuing co-operation. We have every confidence of achieving a safe landing within the next few minutes, and the next time you hear my voice, we'll be saying hello in a bright and comfortable airport lounge."

This is said in such a determinedly cheerful and confident tone, some people break into applause. As if they're already safe; or as if the outcome amounts only to some clever balancing trick. Still, they have done well, to this critical point. Nothing actually brutal has occurred as far as Lila can tell, and it will soon be over.

Now that the moment has come, she misses the waiting. After all, she shouldn't have complained about it; this immediate judgment, fate, event, is surely harder than mere suspension.

She has been wrong about a number of things.

"I feel sick," Tom moans.

"Take deep breaths. Close your eyes."

Not quite yet. First they watch Sheila show them once more how to position their bodies: heads down, hands gripping ankles, if possible. Lila wraps her purse strap over her shoulder and around her body, the purse itself tight under her left arm. Women aren't like men, with all their essentials in pockets. Her purse contains money, passport, identification, the essentials of her existence.

She hopes other women are taking the same care to preserve the necessities.

The heads-down posture must be quite a strain for the large or unfit. Lila is pleased by her own flexibility.

"That's better," says Tom. "You okay?"

"Yes. Thanks." It's hard to talk or even breathe properly, bent double like this, but there must be something to say. Something profound, or summarizing. "I don't regret us, you know," is what comes out. "I'm entirely grateful."

"I know. Me too."

There is still his letter. There is time only for small, sad, upside-down smiles before the plane takes an awful dive, then a terrible leap, and their heads hit the seats in front of them, hard. Lila hears a child, probably Susie, wailing close by.

They are diving steeply and also dancing in the air. When the plane tips to the left, Tom tips into her and she is aware of his shoulder and arm touching her. When he rights himself, she misses him and extends a hand. He reaches out and takes it.

There'll be no warning of ground. She is rigid in anticipation. Tom must be petrified. She can feel the hard bones of his fingers. The skeleton of the plane trembles, its skin bubbles. It's doing its best, and so is she.

Metal is cracking and screeching, the plane's heart is breaking around them. Leaning into soft, long-ago, smooth red velvet, she can only see darkness ahead.

She is flung hard into the air, and the seatbelt grabs at her hips. Her hand flies free of Tom's. The grinding is ear-splitting.

Again she is thrown upward, Tom flying and bouncing beside her, their heads bashing the seatbacks ahead. The plane is shrieking. She could stay bent and blind this way forever, if that's what it takes. Other people's screaming is terrifying, but Lila is silent, beyond jolting breaths. Her body feels as if it's breaking and shaking apart, and it hurts, she hates pain, and here they go, tossed up again. And again, more gently this time.

And again, more gently, and again. Until it stops, and everything is abruptly quiet; perfectly still.

ten

. . . .

GRACELESS AND FLAIL-
ing, Lila hurtles through a long darkness into high, flaring sunlight.

She hurts, in her heart and her head.

The sudden light stabs. She shakes her head, and bits of
knowledge fly upwards, sideways, falling disordered here
and there.

The radiance isn't sunshine at all, it's the shocking
white lights of a great many cameras. Lenses dance on
shoulders straining over barriers all around.

She rolls upright with the help of the outstretched hand
of a stranger. Good thing she wore slacks. It must be too
late to cover her face, but she tucks her head momentarily
anyway into the shoulder of her yellow-rain-slickered
rescuer, who folds a grey woolly blanket around her and
steers her gently, relentlessly forward.

These colours! His slicker is such a brilliant golden yellow, and so shiny, Lila thinks she can see her own blurred reflection. And those red and white whirling lights—are colours always this vivid, and she's just never noticed?

Looking down, she sees even the tarmac is glittering, pitted by small holes in which black shiny rain gathers.

It ought to be smoother. It doesn't look safe.

The moment must be very noisy, she can see people's mouths open, apparently shouting, and a good deal of running about. Maybe it's the trucks and ambulances that create this rhythmic underbeat, thud-thumping in tune with her heart. Otherwise sound is distant, a kind of buzz and whir, like rain.

It *is* raining. Well, they're in England, what else? The grey woolly blanket is getting colder and damper—why is she wrapped up in it, while her rescuer gets a bright slicker? And why are they walking? Wouldn't you think there'd be vehicles to ride in, wherever they're going? Besides those ambulances, she means, and fire trucks.

She could have hidden in an ambulance if she had managed to break something, like a leg.

It looks as if some people did break parts of themselves. There are stretchers, and here and there the men and women carting them about break into a run. The cameras zoom in on them, which is all to the good.

There will be order and patterns in what is occurring, she just can't discern what they are. After that long period of suspension and waiting, events are now going too fast. Not being able to hear properly makes the confusion hard to unravel, as well.

She must be a mess; everyone else is.

They are caught now, she and Tom, wherever he is, in the glare of this happy outcome.

She doesn't much care, and if she did, it wouldn't make any difference.

What will he do with that precious letter of his; will it do him much good? She giggles and the arm around her loosens, then tightens, as if it is nervous.

She bets the man it belongs to has no idea what fear is.

She, on the other hand, must now be in a whole new category: people who know what fear is and what it can do. Is that something to be proud of?

It's certainly different, anyway. She feels herself grinning, and snuffles merrily into her protector's bright shoulder.

Where the hell are they going, and why is it taking so long? She is so very thirsty; she could drink dark water from puddles, sweat from her companion's skin, ice from wings, blood from a stone. She would kill for a coffee, die for a Scotch.

Well no, hardly that.

Suddenly they're passing through a set of automatic doors into a blast of heat and damp-woolly smells, a huge blank grey high-ceilinged room filling rapidly with vivid rescuers and drab rescuees.

So many faces! Some ring a bell, but from what circumstances, exactly? Moisture rises, making the atmosphere steamy.

The smell of coffee is filtering through the air. Shrugging the heavy blanket back off her shoulders, Lila heads for the source, and the yellow arm falls away, too. There are no cameras here.

She's still grinning, and why not? Why isn't everyone? But uneasy people shift out of her path, as if she's the odd one in a room filling with shivering, stunned survivors.

They, too, should get rid of those awful wet blankets.

Isn't this lovely, isn't it kind—thoughtful people have set up a long table with cookies, and glasses of orange juice in rows, and huge urns of coffee and tea. Just the thing.

Lila smiles at a plump woman behind the table, takes a cold orange juice, downs it in a swallow. "Coffee too, please." She can at least hear her own voice, and is gratified that it's steady and firm.

It's a bloody great miracle, this hard, durable floor under her feet. Looking around, she sees yellow-slickered figures moving through the growing crowd like fireflies, and survivors emerging from their blankets to reveal jungle-bird splendours.

Her own flattened reflection in the shining, silvery urn is briefly startling. Doesn't she look younger than when she started out, and wouldn't it make better sense if she looked considerably older? She leans forward, peering, and her features flatten further in the percolator's curve. Her hair is godawful, all over the place.

Her hair is brown. That's why she looks younger, she dyed it last night. She'd forgotten. Just last night. Time is as distorted as reflections in curved, shiny surfaces.

The plump coffee woman looks both concerned and benevolent; the kind of person Lila imagines would be a good mother. Lila would not have been a good mother. For one thing, she lacks the sweet, come-to-my-bosom countenance of good mothers, like this woman.

"Thank you," she says, taking the cup, taking a sip. But it's loaded with sugar, practically syrup, not straight and spine-stiffening the way Lila likes it. "Could I trade this for a black, please?" She offers the cup back. "And is there a bar someplace here? Is there a real drink to be had?"

She can't quite make out the answer, but concentrating on the plump woman's lips, trying to read them, she also can't make out a clear yes or no. The woman is frowning slightly, in a worried, not disapproving, sort of way, and pushes the sugary coffee back, nodding insistently. She has spoken what look like several full sentences before she gestures to someone over Lila's shoulder. Lila supposes she may have one of those accents that are hard to understand anyway, never mind having to lip-read.

Turning, Lila finds a man at her side. He, like the woman, looks earnest and concerned, although lacking her maternal appeal. He's wearing a white jacket, somewhat stained and disordered, and she assumes he's somebody medical. "I can't hear what you're saying," she tells him loudly, as if he's the deafened one. She keeps smiling widely, though, in what ought to be a reassuring way but apparently is not.

Nobody seems as pleased by events as she is. Of course there are flaws, naturally there are. What pleasure is ever quite pure? But they're here, they're alive, and that's as good as a day like this gets.

It doesn't look as if Tom would agree.

It's a shock to see him coming through the door under the guiding arm of his own slickered protector. Her heart leaps at the sight of him, out of habit, or love.

She didn't exactly forget him, but she did somehow forget she is not entirely solitary here.

He isn't grinning, or even smiling. He looks, in fact, decidedly grim. She should be hurrying towards him, arms open.

She sips her sweet coffee. He is a balding, beautifully boned, slightly pot-bellied man whom she has apparently loved mainly for his energies and appetites. Even morose or disgruntled, he has felt big to her, oversized in his desires, wanting much and daring quite a lot.

Now he looks ordinary. Deflated and fretful. Wild-eyed, of course, but who isn't? One arm of his shirt is ripped, and his trousers, like her own, are grimy. He has a bruise on his forehead, which is purple and bleeding a little, but it doesn't look serious.

He looks very serious.

"I would really, very much, like a Scotch right now,"

she tells the white-jacketed man. Through the peculiar din in her head, she makes out a few words: "medical . . . wait" and even "forbidden." Imagine forbidding anything to the people in this room! Surely they are no longer likely to be, if they ever were, people who take no for an answer.

At least she's beginning to catch words here and there. Before she approaches Tom, though, she wants to be able to hear precisely the words he says first, when he sees her alive and uninjured. "Oh my darling, you're safe, nothing else matters, you are the world to me now," she imagines, and hears herself snort. The medical person looks very concerned and reaches out for her arm.

A day like this does not make them children. Quite the reverse, Lila would say. This fellow, whoever he is, knows nothing at all.

She is dazzled by life, amazed by death, and astonished by what the tiny space in between can contain. Parts of her, and not just parts of her body, feel wrenched into unfamiliar shapes and postures. In time they will probably come to feel natural.

She is blessed with time, thanks to the determined struggles of the plane, now abandoned out in the chilly darkness, terribly wounded. How carelessly she hurried away from it the first chance she had. That's very sad. Only, it was a mad scramble, confused and noisy and desperate, and she simply forgot to feel grateful or tender.

Tom, of course, that good man, behaved well.

He is looking around anxiously, presumably for her. Is it cruel of her to take shelter behind a tall back?

Someone else who behaved well was the big man by the emergency exit. As it turned out, he was a cool and orderly figure who must have saved a number of people, including herself, and possibly Tom.

That moment of silence when the plane trembled to its halt was only that: a moment. Then, terrified people scrambling over seats and each other in the sudden darkness, struggling and pushing, discipline and civility, as she'd suspected, mainly vanished.

Tom, gripping her wrist, shoved his own body forcibly into the aisle past pressing bodies and loud voices, pulling her after him, making space for her firmly in front of him. His eyes were narrow, lips tight. Also as she'd suspected, there was no way to make out the emergency lines beneath all the trampling feet.

A voice from the cockpit was only dimly audible in the uproar. Some people shouted, "Let's keep calm, take care," but the message wasn't widely heard or heeded.

Tom, behaving well and sternly, as no doubt other quiet, decent people did, released Lila's wrist and pushed her forward, letting Susie and her mother into line between them. Lila heard a man protesting, Susie and her mother crying, and Tom's hardest, coldest tone of voice. She lost track of him then.

He is a good man. A man who does good. She watches him take a coffee from a woman, with a quick, distressed smile that gets nowhere near his eyes.

Her heart goes out to him, but the rest of her is still unwilling. She isn't ready to deal with his despair; although it's possible this day has transformed his heart, as well, and despair may be the farthest thing from his mind.

It would be difficult, from his bleak expression, to imagine so, however.

The plane's emergency exits opened into tunnels, dark flowers blooming downwards. The big man braced himself against the open space. "One at a time," he commanded. "Go easy, don't push. Efficient and safe, that's what we want." He had a rumbling, chesty sort of voice which, if it didn't exactly stop people in their tracks, at least held authority.

Where was Sheila? Saving lives, maybe, or dealing

with injuries, or overcome. Lila didn't hear anyone question why the big man should take charge, and found she rather wanted, herself, to live up to his demands.

He counted off people with a touch to the shoulder and down they went, into the chute, vanishing into the night. "You there," he ordered someone pushing behind her, "get back and be quiet. Your turn's coming." She felt almost docile, nearly safe. She turned briefly, searching for a glimpse of Tom, but then the big man touched her shoulder, said "Go!" and she slipped obediently past him, onto her ass and down.

Where is he now? "I'll come," he said, "when you've all gone through properly." As if his restraint guaranteed their survival, and as if his appearance would be a reward for their restraint. Who was he before today, and what was he flying towards? No fleeing wife-killer, after all. Was he surprised by himself, taking charge in a critical turn of events, or is that normal for him?

If it's the kind of decisive, stony man he always is, what sort of day-to-day companion would he be? Rather difficult, perhaps.

Lila once had great, if ill-defined, hopes. She sees, peering towards Tom around shoulders and between bodies, that love has been one great thing; if hardly the only thing.

Who else is here? Who else is okay?

She can't spot Sheila, but perhaps the crew was taken elsewhere. They probably have more difficult hours ahead; obviously there will be investigations.

Susie's mother is sitting cross-legged on the floor, against a wall off to Lila's right. Her face is buried in Susie's neck, with Susie curled into her lap, and they are rocking back and forth together. Now there's relief, and joy, and love.

Jimmy and Mel are obviously fine, too. They stand out even in this brightening crowd, all high handsomeness and striking posture. They're twenty steps and a world away from Lila, narrow bodies folded together, heads tipped into each other's shoulders, swaying as if they hear slow music playing.

For all Lila knows, there *is* music playing.

She's happy for them. They're almost certainly among the people here who will make the most of the results of the day.

She's happy for Sarah, too, whom she spots standing over to the left, with a woman bending towards her holding a steaming cup. It's like watching one of those time-lapse photography programs that show a plant growing, unfolding, beginning to blossom. Sarah nods, sips, and slowly, slowly begins to look up, look around, her eyes focusing, her body straightening. Rejoining the land of the living, Lila thinks.

Sarah spots her and grins, a big, wide, full, sudden grin. She raises her fist, a gesture of defiance and victory. Lila grins back, raising hers in return.

This *is* a victory. They have taken part in a triumph.

Sarah's sister will be waiting somewhere in the terminal. Whole different dramas will have been endured by anxious people waiting on the ground. Probably they've been herded into a huge room of their own, to be fed syrupy coffee and careful, hopeful words. In that room, too, there will have been weeping and suspense, some unfortunate behaviour and some acts of virtue, and also, in some instances, no doubt some reconsiderations.

Lila imagines Sarah and her sister will be spectacularly glad to see each other. Soon, Sarah will be jumping with impatience; unless she has changed, too, and no longer speaks whatever comes into her head. Her husband may well find her a surprise when she gets home. Her children may be puzzled.

Lila can't see Adele, but she's little and easily lost in a crowd. Also she is old, and may have been one of those whisked off by ambulance. Her bones could be as brittle as her faith.

"Brittle" is one of those appealing, ambiguous words Lila likes: implying something breakable when referring to bones, but something much harsher in connection with faith.

It's a relief to feel words coming back.

Her hearing, too, is sorting itself out. She can distinguish some individual voices now. "Jesus Christ," she hears. And "How long till we get out of here?" and "I don't have a thing; I can't even prove who I am," and "I swear to god, I'll never fly again." Nearby, a man's sceptical tone: "It probably wasn't even that serious. Nobody tells the truth about anything. I bet they ditched our luggage for nothing."

This, Lila thinks, is a truly impressive cynicism. She has an impulse to say to him, "Asshole." She was a gentler woman, with gentler impulses, when she couldn't hear. She laughs, but only to herself.

A bulky, grey-haired woman barrels through, talking loudly although not to anyone in particular. "Did anybody see what's going on out there? The plane's on fire. I heard there're three people dead, a couple and an old woman. Dead! Never mind how many hurt. My god!"

Is this true?

It could have happened easily in that dark stampede. Briefly, Lila feels herself back there, her own breath being squeezed, her own bones crushed. To have all those hours, and all that fear, desire and grace, turn out fatally—tears finally come to her eyes. It seems they're for everything. Everything.

She hopes the couple was content, being together. She hopes the old woman was not Adele.

She hopes what the bulky grey-haired woman said is not true.

Imagine making it all the way to that moment of stillness, to have life right in your sights, and then to be trampled by frantic fellow passengers also with life right in their sights.

Terrible, too, to know yourself later as one of those with frantic feet.

And the poor plane, getting just as far as it needed to, doing the very best it could, and then not being saved, itself.

So much for Tom's letter. It'll be burned to a crisp.

She laughs again, about that at least, and oh hell, here's that white-jacketed fellow back at her side. "Please, come sit down. We'll get you looked after in no time." Now that she can hear him, she decides his voice has a rather pleasing, lilting cadence. Something northern, nearly Scottish. She smiles at him, but pulls away. "Are you injured?" he is asking. "Are you hurt?"

Hard to say, really. Her soul feels somewhat bashed, if that counts, but she doesn't suppose there's much aid here for battered souls. "Just fine," she says brightly. "I had a little trouble hearing, but that's fixed itself, and now I'm perfectly fine."

"Are you with anyone?"

"Yes, I just spotted him away over there," and she gestures in a direction far from Tom. "If you'll excuse me, I'll go let him know I'm all right, and make sure he is too. I do thank you for your concern, though."

How very kind people can be. She is again suddenly, profoundly, fond of each one here, and very glad to be among them still.

Someone with a microphone is setting out to create order, bringing everyone back to normal life.

There will be those forms to fill out, practical matters to

be dealt with. Spirits will begin to enclose themselves, the trembling of remembered terror will gradually ease. Love and gratitude will lose their most acute, sharp edges.

Strands of people are already forming into structures, patterns of movement are developing, attentions are being gathered up and aimed in one direction.

It turns out not to be very difficult to slip away.

Lila keeps an eye on Tom as she works her way around the edge of the crowd towards an unobtrusive, unmarked grey door. He is a rare, kind, funny, cold-tempered, greedy, generous man who has desired everything, and tried very hard. Now events crash down on him. He looks lost and sad, and also quite worried. He is still trying to manage two things at once.

She would like at least to be able to comfort him, but can't afford to. These moments of clear possibility are rare in a life, as briefly illuminated as strobes or fireflies.

He will be frantic, but although it's cruel, and hardly the same, she has worried at times about him. When he's been out of touch. Off on a trip. Driving through hazards without her. Or at home with his wife.

Later he'll be terribly angry, but there have been times Lila's been angry with him, including today. He will grieve, too, but there have been hours and days when sorrow has emptied her heart.

This isn't vengeance, merely something she knows.

The grey door opens into a very long, grey, narrow corridor. Sliding through, she could still slide back; it's not too late.

Far away, she can see another unmarked door. She feels each step, remembering her yearning not long ago to have her feet on firm ground, heels touching, toes touching, moving forward.

The next door opens into another hallway, and shuts behind her with a click.

The silence now is so impressive it almost feels solid, and she stops for a moment. There are also not many truly silent moments in a life.

In this passage, red arrows have been painted on the walls, pointing only ahead. It still isn't too late, though, never mind locked doors. Nothing is irretrievable yet. She is creating irretrievability, however, by heading towards something which may not be quite familiar, but which is there for her to put her hands to, her mind on. Something touchable.

A day like this is a gift, although a monstrous one.

It turns out, as she pushes open the next door, that she has reached a broad and finally familiar concourse. She's never before been in the customs and immigration hall when it's empty, but the painted lines and signs and booths are recognizable and oddly, comfortingly, homey. She only came at it from an unusual angle, that's all, possibly following the private route of employees or baggage.

Now she knows where she is.

There are arrows and signs for people moving to this country, temporary visitors, people with items to declare and those sailing right through. A woman about Lila's age, in uniform and perched on a stool in one of the sailing-through booths, looks up startled from a book. "Who are you? What are you doing here? You from that plane?" It's obvious what plane she means. "They letting you people through already?" She has grooves at the sides of her mouth, and tiny, withery lines running along her upper lip; surely she looks much older than Lila. Or more weathered. How arduous is her life, when she isn't sitting here?

Lila remembers intending to look up "arduous" and "ardour." Why was that? "They're starting to," she tells the woman.

"There's supposed to be somebody with you. I thought it was going to be ages yet."

"It may be for most people, but I checked out fine and I have everything with me, all my documents, so it was a lot quicker for me. Here's my passport," handing it over. "My ticket."

The woman still looks uneasy. "There's supposed to be staff back there doing identification and claims."

"There are. A lot of people are helping. I'm lucky, getting through so fast. Well"—Lila smiles disarmingly, gratefully—"I feel incredibly lucky all around. Such a day."

The woman nods sympathetically, reminded of what Lila has been through, although, Lila thinks, she has no way whatever of knowing. "Awful thing. I expect you're exhausted."

"I just want to get away, that's for sure. Collect myself. Recover."

"All you have is your handbag?"

"That's all. Others don't even have that much."

"I know. It's going to be a nightmare. You've done the luggage claim?"

"All taken care of." If, tomorrow or the next day, Lila wants to add up and claim her losses, it will irritate and inconvenience the airline people, but that's a small concern. Anyway, a few lost possessions are the least of the matter. Lila catches a flicker of her original holiday vision, then it's gone.

"At least all you lost was luggage." The woman is typing Lila's information into her computer. "Must have been horrid."

Yes, and much more.

Once Tom sorts himself out, he'll probably go to his conference. That will be good for him, in a concerned, angry, grieving sort of way. At least it'll be reasonably easy for him to find out Lila's alive and uninjured.

Thanks to this computer, he won't have to fret about something as basic as that.

There is something about the size and texture of a small rock in Lila's heart when she considers him. She regrets his worry and sorrow, that's all.

"Ma'am?" The woman is looking at her sharply—she must have missed something. "Are you sure you're all right? Were you checked by a doctor?"

"Oh yes, a very thorough and attentive young man." If that white-coated medical person was a doctor, he was certainly attentive, at least. "I just got a few scrapes. And my clothes are pretty much wrecked, as you see. But we heard three people were killed. Do you know if that's right? Do you know who?"

She has succeeded in both flustering and diverting the woman. "Oh. Yes. I believe that's the case, unfortunately. But we're not giving out names until families are notified."

Families. Always families. As if they're necessarily nearest and dearest.

That bitter flash is just an old, bad, irrelevant habit. Bound to happen now and again.

"Only, I heard one was an old woman, and I wondered if it might be someone I had a long chat with on the plane. I didn't see her afterwards, and I've been wondering. Adele Simpson?" Lila also wonders why she's risking her own capture to find out about someone she didn't much like in the first place.

Capture?

Well, she is becoming a fugitive of sorts, that's all she meant.

The woman looks alarmed. "Oh dear. I shouldn't. Don't tell anyone. But that is one of the names. I'm terribly sorry. This is all dreadful, just dreadful." She even reaches out to touch Lila's arm. Another kind person beneath the uniform, after all, another good sign.

Poor Adele, in her prim, print housedress—was she in any doubt, or was she praying joyfully at the end, however it came? Was she very scared, or in pain? Is she already happy in heaven, her reward for an unforgiving life?

"That's too bad," Lila says. "A shame." Because you can't assume people will be happier, or better, elsewhere. Or if they get what they claim to want most passionately.

They may have merely fallen into a habit of passionately wanting, forgetting the roots and origins of their desire.

"I'd better get going." Lila retrieves her passport and ticket. "When the rush starts, you'll be busy."

"Do you know where to go? There's a room where people meeting the passengers are waiting."

"Thanks, but I wasn't being met." The woman looks pitying; Lila may have sounded pathetic. "I was getting together with someone at a hotel in the city." There, that sounds more interesting. And it's true, also. That is what she had been going to do.

"You're sure you're all right?"

"Absolutely. And very glad to be alive." Which is entirely and gloriously true. "Thank you."

After his conference, Tom will go home.

She'll probably go home as well, although she can't imagine the flight, getting back on a plane. Will she be able to?

But two weeks from now—that's infinitely distant, and unpredictable. A past doesn't vanish, but Lila knows how it sorts itself in the memory in swift, unforeseeable ways.

A future takes surprising turns in an instant, as today has made implacably clear.

Boarding a plane may be a very small matter when the time comes.

These steps she is taking on these wonderfully solid floors, these decisions she is making without deciding them—how strange all this is. She feels in the grip of necessity, inexorability. She is moving in the direction of longings she cannot identify yet, but is quite certain of, nevertheless.

I want, she thinks. *I want more.*

She wants brilliance. An electric existence. She wants to make her own hair stand on end.

If she goes on without love of a certain kind, she will still sustain a full heart. She will absorb colours and lights and impressions, and will not put words to them, necessarily. Not every experience will have to make sense; not every action will need to be scrutinized. This seems to her an outcome that is, so far, both acute and calming.

She will ride a motorcycle, and have a rosebud tattooed on her butt.

Tom, less readily amused, will have reached his own conclusions.

She will miss their conversations.

She can't speak for him, he may well feel differently, but she has no desire to uproot love from the organs and veins and small spaces it has twined itself into. This isn't like anger or anguish demolishing love itself. She imagines that what remains of the two of them will be like cleaning up after a party: the event is over, the spirit is fatigued but cheerful, and there are plates and glasses to be washed, some spillages to be mopped and some festive pictures to be appreciated and put away.

That would strike Tom, no doubt, as chilly, and he would be wounded. He prefers warmer visions, rosier words, softer, more pliant conclusions. He thinks they are easier. She thinks that, in the end, they are not.

She was a child who went fearlessly high on a swing, and flung herself free without thought. She feels exceptionally blessed by the chance to do it again.

It's quite simple, walking through the terminal without

the burden of luggage. She is brisk and invisible, a middle-aged woman no one would notice even if they weren't absorbed by concerns of their own. It doesn't matter that she's dented and bruised, and that her clothing is marked and torn—she has acquired the gift not only of being imposing, but also of being unobtrusive, when she desires.

She, on the other hand, notices sounds, movements and most particularly the sweet smell of humans who are merely anxious, not terrified, as if they are knife-pricks in her skin.

So many people at airports embrace for one reason and another, either casually or with passion. That's pleasing to see.

Passing through the final set of doors, she pauses outside on the sidewalk.

Astonishing: there is the huge dark sky she so recently inhabited, tinged with city brightness. From here it's a vast blanket overhead, protective and comforting, giving no hint of its perils, or of the transformations it makes necessary.

A slight, blissful breeze carries genuine, cool, city-stink air. The light rain is no longer chilling, and standing here is a miracle.

"Hey, love," a cabbie calls. "Lift?"

Well yes, she supposes. She can't stand here forever with her feet planted and her face turned up to the sky. "Please," she says, and heads towards him.

"Where you going?"

There's a question, isn't it, and only momentarily a minor, disappointing one. New lives, like old ones, will be mainly made up of small decisions and details.

Certainly Tom's quaint little vacation hotel is out of the question. Somewhere, in fact, quite the opposite.

"I don't have a reservation, but one of the big airport

hotels around here, I think. Do you know one that'll likely have vacancies?"

"Hop in, we'll find you one. Bags?"

"No luggage."

Oh dear, it's tempting to make something symbolic of that, but she resists. It's the first of what she imagines will be many little, sometimes amusing resistances, and some large ones, too.

She feels slightly drunk, heady, out of her skin.

She also looks like hell, and can expect strange glances at the hotel. Even the cabbie looks so wary as she shifts into the back seat that she laughs. Gosh, that makes people nervous. Funny world, when joy and delight are either annoying or scary.

A whole life ended today, she thinks, but that's so pompous, she snorts, earning herself another nervous glance. She's been snorting a lot today, not a very appealing habit.

What on earth is she going to do?

At least she's happy enough with her first decision: a large, anonymous hotel where tonight she can have a drink and a shower and stare out into darkness, and where in the morning she can call for breakfast and coffee, and sit at the window watching airplanes landing and lifting off. In daylight, that should be stirring, even beautiful; a view that could hold her attention for quite some time.

She will become lonely, and can expect to miss Tom.

Eventually, she'll have to get out and buy clothes, everything from underwear to coat and sturdy shoes. She pictures doing a good deal of walking, although not exactly where. She'll also call Patsy and Nell, just as soon as she has enough words.

They've each done mad things in their time, and will no doubt have ideas. Perhaps they'll want to fly over to join her. That would be fun. She'd like to have fun. Would they enjoy motorcycles, would they agree to rose-buds of their own? To going exploring in long, graceful duster coats?

Has she done a mad thing? Like Aunt June, is she step-ping from one side of an invisible line to the other, ex-changing a difficult, pleasing, quite ordinary life for one of increasingly vast eccentricity? She shrugs, alone in the back seat.

Farewells and irrevocable decisions are always un-nerving. Leaping off cliffs, diving with eyes closed, things like that. Fearsome and exhilarating. She may have trou-ble sleeping. She is ravenously hungry.

Eating incautiously, perhaps she'll get fat. Something large, in some respect, seems called for. All her restraints and silences, what were they for?

She can't quite recall.

What she recalls is that, in those hours in the air, she felt most painfully, besides the terror, sorrow at having given in; reconciled herself; forgotten too much. Regret, she supposes. It was a surprise to discover regret.

Also a surprise to discover a capacity for radiance.

"You all right?" the cabbie asks.

Why, was she doing something peculiar?

"I'm fine. I just came in on a plane that was on fire for a while and almost crashed, so I'm still a bit shaky. But fine."

"My god, did you?" His expression alters instantly from wariness to concern and sympathy. "I've got tea if you'd care for a hot drink. Or a blanket, if you'd like that."

What a kind, human desire it is, to warm other hu-mans—it's by no means always a matter of anarchy, is it? "Thank you, but I'll be okay. I feel quite lucky, really."

She wonders if he'd care to join her for a drink. She wonders what events and circumstances made him into a compassionate cabbie offering warmth at the drop of a hat. There are so many stories, some of them about generosity, kindness and virtue. Along, of course, with tales of massacres and cold-hearted rivers of blood, and ill will, and evil.

She imagines the rough and smooth textures of clothes she will buy, and the cool comfort of boots, and stretching her legs. She sees herself taking long strides, covering miles and miles over the earth. The whoosh of the tires on the dark, rainy road is soothing but also very exciting. She feels as she has sometimes done with Tom: as if she could drive through the night forever.

This is hardly how she expected her day to be ending, when she opened the door to him not so many hours ago.

Even so, here she is, going off on her holiday at last.

Since she is headed for something, she observes the details of her progress with keen and superstitious interest. The cabbie is helpful. The seat is wide, and the upholstery is soft, gentle on her bruises. The night is velvet and her spirit is high. These are all very good signs.

It's also true that she's weeping, rather the way Tom did on the plane, without particular movement or sound.

She feels born again, as Adele might have said, meaning something else entirely. She snorts, one last time, as the cab swings towards a hotel lighted wall to wall, floor to skyline. She hopes that at some point Tom will also find something funny, as well as new, about the way today has gone.

When she gets out of the taxi, she finds herself standing under the portico of the high, bright hotel, looking into its busy, anonymous lobby. Where she feels she is standing is at the centre of emptiness, with no sign of horizon. She also sees herself standing far from the centre, balanced on the very edge of invisible, irresistible extremes.